PLANES

PLANES

Peter C. Baker

ALFRED A. KNOPF

NEW YORK

2022

THIS IS A BORZOI BOOK PUBLISHED BY ALFRED A. KNOPF

www.aaknopf.com

LIBRARY OF CONGRESS CATALOGING-IN-PUBLICATION DATA
Names: Baker, Peter C., 1984– author.
Title: Planes / by Peter C. Baker.
Description: New York, NY : Alfred A. Knopf, 2022.
Identifiers: LCCN 2021033591 (print) | LCCN 2021033592 (ebook) |
ISBN 9780593320273 (hardcover) | ISBN 9780593320280 (ebook)
Subjects: LCGFT: Thrillers (Fiction)
Classification: LCC PS3602.A58667 P48 2022 (print) |
LCC PS3602.A58667 (ebook) | DDC 813/.6—DC23
LC record available at https://lccn.loc.gov/2021033591
LC ebook record available at https://lccn.loc.gov/2021033592

Front-of-jacket photograph © Kristin Lee/Getty Images
Jacket design by Linda Huang

Manufactured in the United States of America

First Edition

for Joanna Frieda Mulder,

who improved every page,

and whose love lights the way forward

PLANES

AMIRA

Five days a week she goes to Monti and works in a jewelry-and-clothing shop, doing whatever the owner says. To get there, she rides the bus or walks, depending on the weather and how well she's slept and how much she's already spent on bus fare that week. All the store's regulars know her; she's a part of the place.

Sundays and Tuesdays no one tells her what to do. She has to decide for herself.

Sundays she stays in Esquilino. Cleans the apartment, does laundry in the basement, goes out to buy food, cooks a large pot of something inexpensive and filling for the rest of the week. She could make the food in the pot better—more pleasing—by adding spices, taking more care. It wouldn't cost anything: the spices are already in the pantry, she knows how to use them. But she's not cooking for pleasure. She's cooking because a person has to eat to stay alive. She calls her parents and tries to be interested in her mother's compulsive summaries of all her latest neighborhood gossip. Neither her mother nor her father asks many questions anymore, other than when she might visit next. Always with the implication: When might she come home forever? She walks to the Internet cafe on the corner to write her emails and letters. Pays fifteen cents per page to have the letters printed. The cafe is run by two Somali men. Brothers, she thinks. They offer her tea, and she usually accepts. "But no sugar, please." She is thirty-two years old, about to turn thirty-three.

Tuesdays she wakes early, prays, listens to the radio forecast, packs a bag, and heads out wandering. She leaves Esquilino and crisscrosses the city, riding bus and train lines as far as she feels like going, sometimes all the way to the end of the line, or, on the lines that have no end, past the point where they start looping back on themselves. When she gets off she walks. She needs to be outside of the relentlessly still and empty apartment. She needs to be out of the neighborhood, away from everything that everyone there is thinking of her or might be thinking of her. She needs to be in motion, tiring out her body, just another woman walking down the street, another woman stopping for a coffee.

Every night she follows the same bedtime routine:
She prays.
She changes into her nightgown.
She goes to the kitchen.
She drinks a glass of water.
She refills the glass.
She fills a second glass.
She takes both glasses with her to the bedroom.
She sets the bedside alarm for tomorrow morning.
She goes to the living room.
She checks that the door is locked.
She turns out the living room light.
She walks back to the kitchen, and if tomorrow is a workday, she sets the backup alarm on the counter. She has never slept through the bedside alarm, but if she ever does, she will

lose a day's income, plus risk the anger of the shop owner, Elena, a woman who is cheerful in general but easily over-whelmed by surprises.

She uses the toilet, flosses, brushes, gargles mouthwash, cleans her face, turns out the bathroom light.

She goes to the bedroom and runs through a series of breathing exercises that were shared with her in an email from Ayoub's lawyer, an American woman named Sarah who knows some stilted Italian, which she insists on using in their conversations and most of their emails, despite the fact that her firm employs several competent translators. Some of these breathing exercises involve standing up, others require lying down. *I myself have never been doing much of meditating or anything similar, before. But these meditation have been helpful to me, at my surprise. For that reason I have shared with many clients and many members family of the clients.*

This is the path she knows into sleep. She doesn't dare risk another route. Doesn't dare brush before flossing, doesn't dare set the kitchen alarm before the bedside alarm. She needs sleep so she can work. She needs to work so she can keep their apartment. She needs to keep their apartment so it is here for Ayoub when he returns, so they can have their life back.

At least twice a week she gets woken halfway through the night by cats in the alley. It usually sounds like two cats. They start in a standoff, hissing; she pictures them as boxers circling each other, unsure who will throw the first punch, or when. Then one pounces, unleashing a flurry of yowling and shrieking. She doesn't know if they're fighting or mating or both. She doesn't know if it happens every night, or only on the nights when it wakes her up. She doesn't know when it started. She knows she never heard them before Ayoub was gone. A year or so ago, she mentioned the cats in a letter, asking Ayoub if he remembered them. But none of the letters she received after that contained an answer. Or if they did, it was hidden by a censor's black bars. But an answer might still come: his letters arrive unpredictably, sometimes months after they've been written, sometimes referencing earlier letters he wrote that she never received, or failing to reference letters she sent him long ago.

Whenever she checks the alley in the morning, the cats are gone. She's never actually seen them. To her, they're just sounds.

She tried earplugs once, but the total silence they created sent her attention inward, to the movement of air and blood through her body, making it impossible for her to fall asleep. When the cats wake her, she lies still, does Sarah's breathing exercises, and tries not to worry.

It's Tuesday, but she can't head out wandering at her usual hour. She promised Meryem, her best friend in Esquilino, that she would spend the morning at her apartment helping to prepare a birthday party for Nada, the older of Meryem's two daughters, who is turning four. She suspects that Meryem has the preparations under control—that, really, she invited her over to make her feel needed. She doesn't want to go to the party—she would rather be out walking—but the only thing she wants less is to miss it. To imagine everyone discussing her absence.

First she runs errands. At the post office she mails four letters: one to her senator, one to her deputy, one to the minister of justice, one to the minister of foreign affairs. Each is a slight variation of a letter she has sent many times before, and each will in all likelihood elicit, many months from now, a response that will be a slight variation of one she has received many times before. But she has been instructed by Sarah to continue sending them, and so she does, keeping copies of every letter and every response in a black plastic tub that sits on the kitchen table. *I know it may seem of zero point,* Sarah wrote. *But it is of importance for the creating of a continuing story.*

Next she walks to her landlord's small office, planning to slip the rent check through the mail slot and be on her way. Unfortunately, the landlord's son is inside, scowling at a pile of papers on the desk. At first, she doesn't recognize him. When she last saw him, over a year ago, he was obviously a bored student helping his father out of obligation and obligation alone. Now he is, or wants to be, a serious young Roman moneymaker: complex haircut, leather jacket, massive watch. He beckons her in. What choice does she have?

"Tell me," he says. "Is there any word from Signor Alami?"

"Thank you for asking," she says. His watch looks like it was polished that morning. "I actually received a letter just this week. He's well."

"And everything is fine with the apartment?"

"Yes. Thank you."

"No problems paying? By yourself? It's not too much of a burden?"

"No burden, no." She reaches into her purse, takes out the envelope with the rent check inside, and holds it out.

He ignores it. "It's a big apartment for one person, no?"

"It would be a big apartment for one person, yes."

"You still work in Monti?"

"Yes." She wiggles the check.

"They must pay you well."

"Yes, thankfully." She says nothing about the money her parents wire her each month.

The landlord's son stands up, walks halfway around his desk, and leans against it. Judging from the look on his face, he seems to believe that doing this increases his powers of contemplation. "You know, many people came to us. Many people. I can't say who. I shouldn't. People concerned, you know, about living so close to someone, or even the wife of someone . . . Well. Many people. They said to us, 'Surely you can do something, surely you have the legal authority.' And I said, 'Maybe we do. Maybe we do. But would it be right?' You know, Signora Alami, this is a business. But I do think businessmen should try to do the right thing. I really do."

"Thank you," she says. "I appreciate it."

He shakes his head in a way that seems at first to convey admiration but grows into an expression of disgust. "Honestly, I don't know how you do it. Living here, with these people. What do your parents think?"

On her parents' few visits to Esquilino, they acted as if they'd been somehow teleported out of Italy and into a strange land full of indecipherable people. A place where they had to comport themselves with constant vigilance or risk the loss of her mother's purse, her father's wallet, her jewelry, his watch—and perhaps even their souls. "They like the neighborhood," she says. "They've always liked the neighborhood."

She extends the check a third time, and finally he takes it, plucking it from her while inspecting his watch, as if *she* had been the one wasting *his* time, time he now needs to reclaim before she bleeds him dry with more pointless chatter.

. . .

The moment she enters Meryem's apartment, Nada comes sprinting down the hallway, arms open for a hug. "Amira! Amira! Amira's here!"

"Happy day, little one."

"I'm not little anymore. I'm four."

"Are you really?"

"Yes!"

"Well, maybe you should have some kind of party. So people can celebrate."

Nada widens her eyes. "Amira! This *is* my party!"

It feels good to help Meryem put up streamers and inflate balloons: to help transform the apartment from its everyday state into a celebration. Not for the first time, she imagines her life without Meryem in it. Usually this happens when she's home alone, compulsively force-feeding herself thoughts about how bad things still might get. But now she's not home, she's here, standing on a chair, holding the end of a streamer as Meryem passes her a piece of colorful tape she can use to attach it to a wall. Nada is watching, ready to clap when the job is done. She's glad she came. Walking can wait.

But once the guests start arriving, she cannot shake the familiar sense that everyone is monitoring her. The adults, anyway. Some choreograph their movements through the apartment with the constant goal—she's sure—of never having to speak to her. Others seek her out and corner her so they can announce, quickly and insistently, that they are thinking of her and Ayoub. They ask if there is *any news* of his case, if there is anything, *anything at all,* they can do to help. *How long has it been now?* They ask mostly in Italian, and she alternates between answering in Arabic (as if to insist on her ability to do so) and retreating to Italian, all too aware that, without Ayoub around, her progress with the language is eroding. No one invites her to their children's birthday parties. No one tells her she must come for tea or coffee. Once they've proved to their satisfaction that they are not shunning her, they move away.

She makes a plate of food, becoming more sure with each item she adds that she won't eat, already strategizing about how to abandon the plate without anyone noticing. Looking up, she catches Bouchra, the mother of Nada's best friend—who is also named Amira—staring at her with a look of pure revulsion. She seeks refuge on the balcony, where she enjoys a breath of solitude before the glass door slides open and she is joined by Walid, who is carrying a plate covered almost entirely by a block of cake.

After they exchange salaams, he switches to Italian. "I was thinking I'd be alone out here. But—oh well." He forks into the cake and lifts a piece to his mouth, spilling crumbs onto his belly and beard along the way. "Children. They grow up so quickly, don't they?" He has a child Nada's age; Amira saw her inside, clutching a stuffed elephant and screaming, *I TOLD YOU I TOLD YOU I TOLD YOU—I DON'T LIKE CHOCOLATE ANYMORE!*

"Yes, it's amazing," she says, also in Italian.

"And Ayoub?" He looks disappointed, as if the question had been repeatedly admonished to stay put, then insisted on sneaking out of his mouth anyway.

"What about him?"

He sets his plate down on the balcony ledge. "Is there—I don't know. A trial?"

"No. There can be no trial because there are no charges."

"And his friend from the pizza counter? The Pakistani?"

"I don't know."

Walid flicks his head to the left, then quickly back to center. It's a gesture she has seen him make at the market, where he runs a produce stall. Usually he does it after one of his employees, most of whom are his nephews, has done something that irritates him. "Don't they have to charge him with something, at some point? Perhaps you should contact the consulate, or the Ministry of Justice. They might be able to do something. Especially for a citizen's wife."

"That's a good idea, thank you. Will you excuse me?" She needs to leave before the inevitable sequence of questions about exactly how long they have been married; about whether, upon his return—*God willing*—the clock will reset on the continuous residency requirement of his citizenship application; about whether his citizenship application will even be able to proceed *given everything*. She understands that to immigrants these questions are as natural and unavoidable as talk about the weather. She understands—and still has to leave.

Walid nods sagely, as if blessing her departure, and re-attacks his cake. She leaves her plate on the balcony ledge. Someone else will deal with it.

Back inside, children run and play and shout, parents try to make conversation over the noise, someone needs a bandage. She feels people looking at her. Pretending not to look at her. She wonders who among them complained about her to the landlord's son. Bouchra? Or maybe that was a lie, something the landlord's son made up. If people knew how much their fellow humans were making things up, she sometimes thinks—if they knew the extent to which the world around them was the product of lies and guesses and unearned confidence—it would break them. Nada careers past, waving something colorful in the air, singing a song:

I'm four now
I'm four now
I'm four now-now-now-NOWWWWWWW
And I'll be. Four. This. Whole. Year!

She has to go. She finds Meryem, who doesn't protest or make a fuss, just thanks her for coming and gives her a firm hug. Meryem's always giving her firm hugs, as if she knows she's starved for affectionate contact. Ayoub has been gone for two years and two weeks and one day. He has spent more of their marriage away than at home, more of it in prison than free. She has lived in Esquilino, in their apartment, longer without him than with him. Walking down the steps to the street, she imagines news of her departure traveling through the party. *She's left. Amira's gone. She's gone.* She can see them all shaking their heads in a collective performance of pity. *Poor Amira. Poor woman. Poor thing.*

Later, while she's cooking, her mother calls and right away starts going on about her butcher: he's too old, his hands shake, he takes too long with everything, with getting the cuts right, with wrapping them up, everything. The lines are longer than ever, she says, and, what's worse, it's not safe, he's going to cut himself or maybe even lose a finger—why would he want that? Why doesn't he let his sons take over?

"Well, Mama, it sounds like he should let his sons take over," she says. Ayoub worked at a butcher stall in the market, before, so her mother's talk of butchers is confusing. It feels like she is, not for the first time, trying to say something about Ayoub without actively saying it. But what?

"What are you doing?" her mother says. "What's that noise?"

"I'm cutting an onion. You're on speakerphone."

"I ran into Paolo Orlandi at the market. He's living in Rome now, can you believe it? I told him to look you up."

She puts the knife down. "What did you say? Why would you do that?"

"Why not? Don't get upset. I didn't do anything wrong. He was home for his mother's birthday, isn't that nice? I told him the name of your store so he could stop by."

"I don't even know Paolo Orlandi."

"Don't be silly, of course you do. You went to school together."

"That doesn't mean I *know* him. Why would you tell him to come to the store? That's just—it's not—"

"Not what?"

"I just wish you hadn't."

"Well, how could I have known that? What do you want me to do? Call his mother and say, 'I'm sorry, you need to tell Paolo not to look up Maria—not to look up Amira—she doesn't actually want to see him'?"

"Let's just change the subject."

They talk another half hour, mostly about the butcher and his sons. By the time they're done, her soup is simmering on the stove.

The next day at work she spends her whole shift fretting that Paolo is about to walk in the door.

They were never really friends, or even part of the same circles. But her mother was right: going to school with someone put you in touch with something fundamental about them that you couldn't know any other way. She would probably feel she knew something about him even if nothing had ever happened between them. She would probably still remember him as a tall boy with a soft, slightly pudgy body of a type that easily could have made him a target for teasing, or worse. But he never got teased, at least as far as she knows. Now that she is thinking of him for the first time in years, she remembers how content he always seemed. He had a toothy grin and he grinned a lot.

They had likely spoken no more than twenty sentences to each other until, just a few weeks before graduation, they ended up talking at a party at Camilla Russo's parents' house. There was prosecco and crisscrossing strands of lights strung up across the backyard, and it seemed to her that the social rules by which she and her classmates had been living for the last several years—all the hierarchies and dividing lines—were starting to dissolve and drift away, up into the early-summer sky. The world was less set than it had been as recently as that morning, and she felt this truth fizzing its way around the party, making people see themselves and each other differently. People who had barely spoken for years were laughing uproariously together. Were spotted heading off together hand in hand in search of privacy. Whatever she and Paolo talked about that night—graduation? the summer? the future?—the real subject was this contagious atmosphere of change. When he leaned in to kiss her, she was shocked and not shocked; it was completely unexpected, but fit perfectly with the mood of the night. He was a good kisser; she hadn't kissed many people, but she knew. They went behind a tree at the edge of the backyard and pressed against each other clumsily but happily and kept kissing and pressing until Camilla's mother called for everyone to gather for a group picture. She didn't want to stop with Paolo but didn't want to miss the picture; as the flash went off, she could still feel the press of his right hand on her left breast. Afterward, the social currents of the evening—his friends, her friends—conspired to keep them apart, and she thought maybe that was the end of it. A few minutes behind a tree. She didn't mind. It didn't feel cheap or bad. It was something special and strange they'd been drawn into together by the forces of change.

A few days later, some of her classmates invited her to a day at the beach in Pescara. It was Camilla Russo's party all over again. These classmates weren't people she knew particularly well. But now that they were no longer forced to see each other five days out of every seven, they evidently felt so close to her that they almost begged her to join them. She couldn't deny it made her happy. Her parents were different now too; they asked none of the usual skeptical questions about exactly who she was going with, what exactly they would do, when exactly she would get back . . . Instead, they seemed just as pleased as she was. "Of course," her mother said. "Go! Go!" On the way they put the windows down to feel the wind and sun on their hair and faces and sang along loud to the radio.

She had no idea Paolo would be there. But then they arrived and there he was, just down the beach with some friends. For a while she just watched him. When he took his shirt off to go swimming, she studied his naked torso. Later, after their groups merged, they ended up sitting together. They found ways to touch each other's bare skin. A finger, a hand, leg grazing leg. When everyone else was swimming and they were alone, he told her that a friend of his older brother's had an apartment that he let them use during the day if they left some wine or beer in his fridge. Did she want to get lunch sometime soon and go see it?

She understood this as an invitation to make love, and she accepted. He was her first, and he said she was his, and she believed him. She loved his body and his easy relationship to it—how, when they were together, the relationship extended to her body, too, making her feel completely at home in herself for the first time. Paolo always brought the bottle of wine. Always, before they left, they stripped the sheets from the bed and put them in Paolo's older brother's friend's laundry basket. That was the best they could do: going to the laundromat felt too risky, and so did buying sheets of their own. One night that magical summer, she met Paolo's older brother's friend at a party; she wasn't sure he realized who she was, but she still felt a bizarre intimacy, almost as if she'd made love with him, too, or might make love with him someday in the future. That was how everything felt that summer: anything was possible, the air itself was thrilling just to touch.

From the start she knew she would not fall in love with Paolo; at the same time, to her, *making love* was the best of the available terms to describe what they did in bed. At the end of the summer they spent one last long afternoon together. They knew it was over: Paolo was staying in Avezzano to figure out what he wanted to do next, and she was headed to Rome for university. She never seriously reconsidered. Part of her suspected that knowing she was leaving had made the summer's happiness possible—and that if she stayed, it would curdle into something sour. They cried a little when they said goodbye, but they were mostly tears of happiness for what they'd managed to share.

She never saw him again. For years, on visits home, she got the feeling that she was going to run into him at the market, on the bus, on the street. Perhaps, if she'd been a different type of person—the type who kept up with everyone from school—she would have known what he was getting up to. But she kept in touch with no one from school. She came back only to visit her parents, not because of any particular attachment she felt to Avezzano. She was a Roman now, like she'd always wanted. Before her mother mentioned Paolo on the phone, she hadn't thought of him in years. And now she's thought of him for most of a workday. Worrying that he's about to show up. Remembering the apartment and what they did there, telling herself that these memories do not make her a bad wife.

For a long time, one way she coped with Ayoub's absence was by shutting out, or trying to shut out, thoughts of anything other than Ayoub: the fact of his absence; what she might possibly be doing to facilitate his return; how to keep their apartment; what had happened to him or possibly happened to him or might yet happen to him. Thinking about anything else felt like treachery. But she has learned to accept that thoughts come and go—that an endless stream of wildly varied thoughts is a defining aspect of being alive, and that alive is exactly what Ayoub needs her to be. All manner of thoughts will exist inside her head, but all that matters is what she does. All that matters is holding on—to the apartment, yes, but also to herself, to life—until Ayoub returns and they can move forward, together, again.

On Tuesday, after she's walked for hours, she decides to sit at a coffee bar and order a cappuccino in her husband's honor.

On one of their earliest dates, the third or fourth, he took her to the Appian Way Park, the Tor Marancia section. During the bus ride, and even more so once they arrived, he was visibly proud to be showing her—a native Italian—a piece of Rome she didn't know. Afterward, they sat in a charming nearby coffee bar with outdoor seating. Even though it was already late afternoon, Ayoub ordered a cappuccino. When the waiter sniggered, she felt a mix of pity and embarrassment. But Ayoub wasn't bothered. He couldn't help it, he explained, he loved cappuccino too much to limit himself to having it only in the morning, the way "real Italians" did. "They can call me a dumb Arab if they want," he said. "They can laugh. But I know I'm a dumb Arab with a delicious drink. Sorry if I embarrassed you, though."

"No," she said. "Not embarrassed." Saying the words made them true. She called the waiter back and changed her order to a cappuccino. From then on, late-in-the-day cappuccinos were one of their rituals. At the coffee bar by the Appian Way Park, they became friendly with the owner, who cheered them on. "Maybe you Arabs could teach us something about being Italian," he said. "If everyone was like you, I could sell cappuccino all day and make more money." *Arabs.* Plural. They never corrected him, opting instead to smile softly at each other and enjoy the moment. Now each cappuccino she drinks alone is money she could be putting away toward rent. She knows that. But she needs to keep the ritual alive.

She's walking home when her phone starts to vibrate in her purse. SARAH LAWYER OFFICE. It takes her more than one try to accept the call, her hands are shaking, she keeps missing the button.

They have a system. Sarah uses it with many of her clients. For most updates, she uses email. If she has information that is not urgent but, for whatever reason, cannot go in an email, she sends an email or text proposing three possible times for a call. She makes unscheduled calls only if she has truly urgent news, news she knows Amira needs to hear right away. The threshold for *needs to hear right away* has never been defined, and Sarah has crossed it only twice. The first time was to tell her that Ayoub seemed to no longer be in Pakistan—but that no one knew where he was, or why. The second time was two weeks later, to tell her that, apparently, he'd been held by the Pakistani secret police but was now almost definitely in Morocco. It was in this conversation that Amira first heard the words *Temara Prison*. Until then, she'd thought it most likely he was lying in a hospital where for some reason they couldn't identify him, maybe his wallet had been thrown from his body in a car crash and he wasn't yet conscious. Sarah's system is supposed to save her clients stress by reducing the number of times they have to hold a ringing phone in their hands, suffocating under the weight of every terrible thing they might be about to learn, all the possibilities they cannot help having read about in the newspapers or online, plus all the permutations of those possibilities their minds can't help generating. The system is also supposed to make it less stressful to check (or not check) email: one can always know that if it's something truly urgent, Sarah will already have called.

She leans against a lamppost. Whatever she is about to learn, dozens of people walking down the street will witness her learning it.

"Hello, Khadija?" It's Sarah, but for some reason she's speaking English.

"Excuse me?"

"Khadija, can you hear me? It's Sarah."

"No, this is Amira."

"Amira? Oh God, I'm—"

"What is it? What happened?"

"No, nothing, Amira." She switches to her broken Italian. "It is a nothing. I'm sorry. I call the wrong number. I mean to be calling someone else. I am sorry, so sorry, very extra sorry. There is no information that is new. I am so sorry. I am . . . tired. I make a mistake. I am sorry."

"Oh." The sickening chemical collision of relief and panic in the gut.

"I am tired and I call the bad number. The not-right number."

"That's okay. It's okay, Sarah. Khadija is . . . another client? The wife of another client, I mean?"

Sarah sighs. "Yes, the wife of a client."

On the way home she cannot stop herself from going into the Somali Internet cafe and googling: *Khadija rendition wife; Khadija rendition Sarah Mayfield; Khadija CIA rendition; Khadija Guantanamo; Khadija husband Guantanamo; Khadija husband Temara.* She finds nothing—nothing she hasn't seen before, nothing specific to Khadija, whoever she is. She should stop but she doesn't: *Ayoub Alami; Ayoub Alami Temara; Arsalan Pakistan prison; Arsalan CIA detained.* And so on. Until she can't bear it.

She has an email from Mourad, Ayoub's best friend from childhood, asking the same questions he always asks in his emails: if there is any news, if there is anything he can do, if she needs money (though he never puts it so directly), if she wants to come and stay with his family in Madrid, for any amount of time. *I know Ayoub would do anything for me, and I will do anything for him.*

At work a fat gray tabby cat sneaks in and starts darting around the store, hiding under the tables, winding between the display racks. The creature seems to delight not just in getting as much hair as possible on the clothes but also in being observed by people who disapprove but are powerless to stop it. Elena grabs a broom and chases the cat around for several minutes until she's winded. "You try," she says, handing Amira the broom. "I'll hold the door open." When they finally manage to shoo the thing out, Elena asks her to identify all the clothes with cat hair on them, take these clothes to the back room, and use a lint roller to remove as much hair as she can. "I would help," she says. "But I'm allergic."

Amira is allergic too. Elena knows this, or at least knew it at one point. Three years ago, not long after she'd been hired, they brought in a cat for a few days to clear up a mouse problem, and they talked about it then. But she decides to keep quiet rather than risk losing points in the tally of her workerly virtues Elena may or may not be keeping in her head. She doesn't think she is remotely close to being fired, but she doesn't want to do anything that could increase her chances, fairly or otherwise. In the back room she puts the hairy clothes on a table and gets to work. Within a minute her throat is tightening up. Within two minutes her eyes are leaking tears. It feels good to have an excuse to cry a little without being allowed to break down sobbing.

"Amira?" It's Elena, peeking in from the hallway. "Are you okay?"

She blinks, smiles. "Yes, I'm fine. Thank you."

"There's someone here to see you."

"Who?"

"I don't know. A man. He's very handsome."

She has told Elena very little about her life outside the store, and her boss looks pleased by her sudden involvement, however tangential, in a potentially juicy story: Amira and the Man. Tearful Amira, Who is Married, and the Handsome Man. "If you want to take a little coffee break . . ."

Thanks to how often Elena makes commentary on the looks of men who come through the store to buy gifts for wives, for girlfriends, for mistresses, Amira knows the range of types that her boss considers handsome, and it does not include bodies that are soft and slightly pudgy the way Paolo's eighteen-year-old body was soft and pudgy.

But it has to be Paolo. Of course it does.

She wonders if his appearance has changed—if he became one of those formerly pudgy men who throw themselves into going to the gym, jogging, cutting out pasta, all to escape their younger bodies. To prove that childhood is not their destiny. To become, physically, the kind of man that women like Elena call handsome.

Right before she crosses from the back room into the store, it occurs to her that instead of Paolo, it might be someone from the Ministry of Foreign Affairs, or the Ministry of Justice.

It's Paolo. When he sees her, he breaks into his same old toothy grin. *Handsome* probably isn't the exact right term, but she can see why Elena used it.

"Amira!" he says. "It is Amira, right? Your mother told me you're Amira now. She was very strict with me about it, she told me not to forget. I hope it's okay that I came by."

"Of course. I have a short break."

And just like that she and Paolo Orlandi are walking down the street together. He talks quickly, like he's nervous, talks about working in a restaurant nearby, how he wants to be a chef but isn't ready yet, for now he mostly helps to make the pasta dough and cut the vegetables, even wash the dishes, it's a small place, so everyone has lots of jobs. He likes restaurant work, he says, wants to stick with it and become a chef, maybe even open his own place if he can figure out the money side, he's committed to working with food but about Rome he has doubts, he's had a hard time feeling at home in the city, it's only been a few months, he knows that, but he feels he's made no progress in building a sense that he might belong here, or that he could possibly stay for the long term. He isn't sure what it is about the city or about himself that is to blame. People keep telling him to *give it time, give it time—* but the feeling doesn't go away. "Honestly, it's good to see a familiar face," he says. "A face from home. I'm sorry that I'm talking so much. I guess I'm keeping these things bottled up and then I saw you and it all just—I'm sorry, I'm being so rude, and it's your break. Are you hungry? Should we be getting you food? I'm being rude, I'm sorry."

She tells him she's fine, she doesn't need to eat. Right away he launches back into it, talking about how, before coming to Rome, he worked at a restaurant in Avezzano owned by one of his uncles, how it was forced to close, which was the scary thing about restaurants, sometimes they just didn't work out, and there wasn't always an obvious reason. The uncle moved to America because his wife got a job at a university there, they live in Chicago and the uncle spends his days tinkering with recipes for the next restaurant he hopes to open, once they've moved back, though who knows if they ever will . . . Paolo goes on like this, telling her about dishes from his uncle's restaurant that he misses making, the high rent in Rome, how he shares an apartment with five other guys and doesn't even have his own room, but fortunately his room-mate is mostly out at night, so at least he gets some privacy when it's time to fall asleep, that's when privacy matters most, to him anyway, he doesn't know about anyone else . . .

As they walk, she makes sure they move in a circle through the neighborhood, one that returns her to the shop in good time. "Oh no!" he says when he realizes that they're almost back. "Does this mean you have to go?"

She nods.

He groans. "But all I've done is babble. I'm sorry, Amira. We didn't even get to—I mean, your mother told me . . . and I heard . . . about your husband, I mean—"

"It's fine," she says. "Really, Paolo, it's fine. I'm glad you stopped by." She's telling the truth. It's not just that, as he said, it's good to see an old familiar face. To have someone unload their worries on you can be a kind of gift. It's a way of saying, implicitly: *You and I are people who can understand each other, whose worries and problems can meaningfully coexist.* No one has unloaded their worries on her for a long time.

"Should I come by again? Maybe on your lunch break someday?"

"No."

"Oh," he says. "I didn't—"

"No, it's just, my boss. She's a bit strange. A bit . . . gossipy, I mean. So—"

"Ah."

"I just—"

"Say no more," he says. "I understand. It's fine."

"But I—"

"I understand, you don't have to—"

"But I could give you my phone number."

That toothy grin! Most of the time, the sight of other people taking simple, direct pleasure from life produces in her an equal and opposite sense of alienation: a sense that she is watching life through a thick pane of cloudy glass. On a bad day, alienation is just the start, the spark that lights a flame of resentment that threatens to melt her down from the inside. But Paolo's toothy grin sends her toward neither alienation nor resentment. She finds herself grinning back.

"So, who is he?" says Elena when she's back inside.

"No one. An old friend."

"Okay. That's fine. Keep your secrets."

When she gets home that evening, there is, for the first time in months, a padded Red Cross envelope in her mailbox. The Amira of two years ago—maybe even the Amira of six months ago—would have run upstairs right away, ripping open the envelope as she ran. But tonight she moves at a normal pace. Even when she's inside the apartment, she takes her time, letting the envelope sit on the kitchen table while she pees, washes her face, pours a cup of water. She has accepted that the letters are guaranteed to say nothing new of substance. *I miss you, I am thinking of you every day, I am looking forward to seeing you again. Sometimes I* ███████████████████. *I wonder if* ███████████████████████████.

And yet, staring at this new letter from across the kitchen, she feels the desire to rip it open building within her, pushing against her from the inside like helium against the interior skin of a balloon. She picks up the phone to call Meryem. After the last time she got a letter, she talked to Meryem about it, trying to describe the experience of opening them, how sad and tired and alone they made her feel. Meryem took her hand and told her to call the next time she got one. "I'll come over as soon as I can," she said. "Then you won't be alone."

She starts dialing but pauses halfway through. She cannot help wondering: To what extent did Meryem's offer come from a desire to make her life more bearable? And to what extent was it about curiosity? To what extent was Meryem looking, consciously or not, for an opportunity to dip into someone else's raw sadness, protected by the knowledge that she would soon be safely back at home with her husband and children?

She hates thinking this way. She puts the phone down and opens the letter: first the outer Red Cross envelope, then the flimsier inner one, on which Ayoub has written her address. She knows before she has the letter out that it will smell of Temara—mold, piss, shit, darkness—and knows that no matter how many times she resniffs the letter, she will be unable to tell if the smell is really on the paper or if it has been placed there by her imagination.

Dear Amira,

I am thinking of you even more than usual today, because ██ ██████████████████*. Yesterday it rained. A man down the hallway from me* ███████████████████████████*.*
Sometimes when things like this happen, it feels like I will be here forever. Sometimes I cannot remember how long I have been here. It seems like I just arrived only yesterday.

God willing, this will be over soon. I am sorry for the pain that

*I know my situation must be bringing you. Someday I hope it
will be a distant memory.*

████████████████████████████████████

████████████████████████,

*Your husband,
Ayoub*

The letter is, like all of his letters, written in Italian. She
has no way of knowing if he does this for her benefit, or
in hopes of stymieing the censor. There is no indication
of when it was written. It tells her nothing. It does worse
than tell her nothing: it takes Ayoub—her Ayoub, the real
individual—and overwrites him with an infinity of possible
Ayoubs, each Ayoub changed forever by whatever he has had
to endure, whatever he is still enduring (potentially right at
this very moment), whatever he might yet have to endure
in the future. Reading the letters makes Ayoub feel farther
away. Not to read the letters would feel wrong—would, in the
end, also make Ayoub feel farther away. Writing responses of
any substance feels dangerous: Who knows who would read
what she said, and what use they could put it to? Writing letters of no substance feels painful. Every day, no matter what
she writes or doesn't write, no matter what she does to keep
their life intact, Ayoub is farther away.

She puts the letter back in its envelopes and takes it to the
spare room—the room where her guests would stay if she
ever had guests, and where their child would sleep if they
had a child. Sometimes she misses this nonexistent child. A
child would tell her what to do next: *Take care of me.* Each
thing she did for the child would also be, unambiguously,

something she was doing for Ayoub. But just as often she is sick with relief that no person is growing up dependent on her, absorbing through the air of the apartment her daily struggle to keep herself from screaming because she knows that once she starts screaming she won't stop.

She puts the letter in the shoebox with the others, lowers herself to the floor, lies flat on her back, looks at the ceiling, and does a breathing exercise: empties her lungs by blowing out through her mouth, inhales through her nose for four seconds, holds her breath for seven seconds, empties her lungs by blowing out through her mouth . . .

If she had a child, this is the ceiling the child would look at every night. This is the window the child would see light coming through. The child would have no memory of Ayoub. She would show the child pictures and say, first in Italian and then in what is left of her Arabic: *father.*

*　*　*

On a Saturday morning in July—her last Saturday on earth as a thirty-two-year-old—she sits at the kitchen table and writes out a note. *Ayoub, I'm at my parents' house. You can use the phone to call me there. The number is on the fridge.—Amira.* She leaves the note on the floor, just inside the doorway. It's not that she actually thinks he will return while she's gone; Sarah has explained that, when the time comes, they will have several days' notice. But leaving a note makes her feel better. What she would really like to do—because surely he doesn't have his keys anymore, surely they were taken from him somewhere along the way and won't be returned—is pin a note on the front door of the building. *Ayoub, I'm at my parents' house. You can use the phone to call me there. Meryem has a spare key for you.* But she can't bear the prospect of anyone seeing the message: soon the whole neighborhood would hear.

After work, she takes a bus to Termini station and buys a ticket for Avezzano.

As always, her mother cooks all of her childhood favorite dishes, more than she could ever eat; she keeps Amira constantly in sight; she assumes they will spend every minute possible in each other's sight; she asks more than once—in the tone of someone asking for the first time—if Amira's sure she can't stay two nights instead of one, if she needs anything to eat, if she wants to do a puzzle or play cards. It all resembles enthusiasm, but she cannot avoid feeling that her mother is looking forward to the moment when she is back on the train to Rome—that the visit is, for her, a burden that second by second becomes heavier and more difficult for her to bear, even threatening her ability to breathe. "You're sure you can't stay another night?" she says again. "You have to go back? You're sure?" They sing for her birthday. One more candle than last year.

Because she's home, she prays every prayer. She has never been particularly strict about the prayer schedule, in large part because Ayoub himself was never particularly strict about it. At her parents' house, though, she prays them all, or tries to. Kneeling on the floor of her childhood bedroom, she cannot avoid being aware of her mother's presence in the house. Sometimes this makes her want to recite the prayers louder, so loud it's impossible for anyone in the house to ignore, just as it is impossible for her to ignore that they are listening. Sometimes it makes her want to pray as softly as possible, insisting on her privacy. Unlike at home, the ritual gives her no peace.

With her father things are easier. After years of debate with himself, he has recently subscribed to a premium channel that gives him access to what appears to be every football game on the entire planet. He can watch all day, if he wants. On Sunday, while her mother prepares a large afternoon meal—a completely new meal, despite the leftovers from the night before—she sits with him in front of the television and listens to him murmur efficient explanations of all the little currents of backstory and built-up stakes she would otherwise miss. Executing this task seems to give him great pleasure. Things are probably different between the two of them than they would be had she never met Ayoub. But how? She can't say, and this is a comfort: she doesn't feel that they have lost each other, or that either one of them is groping to retrieve some old or imagined version of the other. When she tells him she has to pray, he pauses the game, which is possible thanks to a digital recording box that came with the upgrade to the premium football channel. For a few minutes after she returns, they're not watching live anymore, they're in the past—until a break in play comes and they're able to fast-forward into the present.

"Don't let me interrupt," says her mother, passing through on her way to the bathroom. "I'm not here." As soon as they hear the bathroom door latch, her father gestures for her to come closer. He reaches into the front right pocket of his favorite cardigan—when she imagines her father, he is always in this cardigan—and pulls out a small envelope, which he presses into her hand. "Put it away, put it away," he says, holding up a finger to his lips and winking.

After the game, she announces that she's going for a walk.

"Alone?" calls her mother from the kitchen. "Are you sure?"

"Of course I'm sure. What do you think's going to happen to me?"

"I'm not saying anything. I'm asking a question."

All through her walk, she feels sure she is about to run into someone she knows. But the only people out are people her parents' age walking dogs. The neighborhood has changed: there are fewer children, or at least that's how it seems to her tonight. To the extent that she can begin to imagine a life where Ayoub never comes back, what she imagines is this: she moves back in with her parents, she cares for them as they age, she buys a dog and walks it, she never goes back to Rome again, never sets foot in Esquilino for the rest of her life. She cannot see her way to any other possible response. She will cease to be a Roman, cease to be a wife, cease to know herself as anything but her parents' daughter. Ayoub used to talk about *flat men*: immigrants who, like him, had been in Italy for years but who, unlike him, had failed to build lives there. These men weren't bums, weren't homeless, didn't drink themselves to death. They kept themselves groomed. They functioned. But they didn't marry or have children, and just looking at them—at their eyes—you could tell that the psychological muscles they once used to connect to the world had atrophied. This is what she would become: a flat woman. A woman with dead eyes walking her little dog. It's a terrifying outcome to contemplate, in part because of how painful it sounds, but more because she feels some reflex inside of her surging toward the pain for the simple reason that it represents change.

Her job isn't to deny these feelings when they come. Her job is to let them come, notice them, and keep going.

She doesn't realize that she's approaching Camilla Russo's parents' house (or the house that used to be their house—she has no idea if they still live there) until it's right in front of her. It isn't possible to see into the backyard—there's a wall—but she can almost feel the prosecco bubbling up inside young Maria, Paolo's lips on young Maria's lips, Paolo's right hand on young Maria's left breast. Young Maria was her, or became her; it feels too outlandish to be true, but there's no plausible counterargument.

At mealtime she's not hungry: her body is still trying to understand what to do with last night's influx of home cooking, so unlike what she makes herself at home, so much cream and cheese and meat. But she knows from past experience that it's best not to turn down her mother's food, and so she loads up her plate and gets to work.

"Did Paolo ever stop by the store?" her mother says.

"No," she says. "Never." The thought of discussing Paolo now, with her mother, is unbearable.

"He shouldn't have said he would stop by unless he meant it."

"Maybe he moved," offers her father. "Didn't you say he was having a hard time with city life? Maybe he had enough. There's no shame in that. What kind of wine is this?"

Her mother shakes her head slowly from side to side. "No. I saw his mother just a couple days ago. She would have told me. It's a new type of wine with less alcohol—do you like it?"

"I can't say that I do, no. But I don't suppose I get any say in the matter, do I?" He seeks Amira's gaze and, when he finds it, winks.

"Do you think," says her mother, "that he told his mother he was going to visit and then she told him not to?"

"Why would she do that?" says Amira.

"You know what people are like. About things."

"No," she says. "I don't. What are people like about things?"

"Don't be difficult. You know what I mean—don't pick on me."

"He might have moved," says her father. "We can't rule that out."

"It doesn't matter," says Amira. "What does it matter? I don't even know Paolo Orlandi, not really."

"Sure you do," says her mother. "You went to school together."

She lies on the floor of her childhood bedroom and runs half-heartedly through some breathing exercises. So many times she lay here, dreaming of real life—or a vision of real life she'd cobbled together from movies and the stories told by her friends' older siblings: living in Rome, exploring the city, going out dancing, attending softly lit gatherings of interesting people, falling into and out of and back into love. She can hear her parents talking at the kitchen table but can't hear what they're saying. She imagines it is about her, and she lets herself remember—it's easier with a wall and shut door between them—that they love her and worry about her and, like her, have been forced to make a life around conditions they never could have predicted.

Her phone buzzes. It's a text, from Paolo: *how's being home?*

They've seen each other maybe a dozen times. Always in Monti. Always on days when she's already in the neighborhood for work. Sometimes on her lunch break. Sometimes after she's done with work. They meet away from the store and walk down the smaller streets of the neighborhood. Sometimes they stop at a bench and sit—always on a bench meant for three people (or more), always keeping a person-sized space between them. Often he comes from the restaurant, where he's helped to prepare for the evening dinner rush, and on these days he brings food: breads, disposable cups of soup, delicate fried vegetables wrapped in foil. He never brings anything with pork in it, a fact that neither of them has ever mentioned. Sometimes they set up their next meeting while parting ways; other times they make plans later, by text. They don't call each other. They don't discuss not calling each other. Often his clothes and even his hair have a dusting of flour from the restaurant; he wears an apron and cap, he says, but they don't do much. Without ever discussing it, they never meet more than twice a week.

After their third walk together, she decided to tell Meryem all about it, to prove there was nothing remotely inappropriate happening. But she quickly realized that, as a matter of logic, telling Meryem wouldn't prove anything. And so she said nothing. What matters isn't what anyone—Meryem, her parents, anyone—would think, watching or hearing about the situation from the outside. What matters is the truth. And the truth, she feels very strongly, is that she and Paolo are people who grew up together and enjoy talking. His compulsive babbling from their first meeting proved to be an anomaly. His normal speech is completely unhurried. He asks plenty of questions. She talks at least as much as he does, maybe more. They talk about the little ups and downs of work. They talk about Avezzano: about their old teachers and classmates and neighbors, what happened to everyone, whose parents are living and whose are dead, who drinks too much, who is married and who is divorced, who is healthy and who is ill, who stayed, who moved away, and who moved back. They talk about restaurants, about food, about Rome, about whether he should stay, when he should decide, how he will know. He asks about her earliest days in the city, and answering makes her life feel like a story with motion, not a picture trapped in a still frame.

They talk about Ayoub, too. When she imagines telling Meryem about these after-work walks and meetings—when she imagines her friend's face becoming more skeptical the more she hears—she imagines herself saying exactly this: *We talk about Ayoub, too!* Somehow Paolo is able to ask questions—about Ayoub, about her conversion, about Esquilino—without making her want to flee, to get back to her apartment, to lie on the floor and never have to answer (or even hear) another question about her husband ever again. They talk about Morocco, and about how strange it is for her to have no firsthand experience of the country where her husband spent the first twenty years of his life. They even talk about his trip to Pakistan—just briefly, but still. Somehow when Paolo asks her a question, she knows for sure that he is asking because he is genuinely interested, not because he is desperate to take her answers and plug them into a template. People use templates, she has come to realize, so they can spare themselves contact with the complexity of the world. Of people. Of life. Insert a variable or two and the template supplies the rest of the story. She knows how her meetings with Paolo might look from the outside: the templates an outside observer would apply, the conclusions they would get, the judgments they would form. She doesn't care. She has the right to something in her life untouched by anyone's perspective but her own.

"If we run into anyone from Esquilino," she says, "I'm going to say you're my cousin. I don't need the gossip."

They haven't talked about what happened that summer, not even tangentially, and not even by suggestion or innuendo.

"Okay, cousin. If we run into anyone from the restaurant, I'm going to say you're a wealthy heiress who invests in exciting new restaurants by talented young chefs."

"Promise?"

"Promise."

Until now, neither of them has ever texted the other for any purpose except deciding when and where to meet. It's not a rule, because they've never discussed it, but still she feels the buzz of transgression as she types back from her childhood bed: *it's okay. parents driving me crazy.*

He responds: *driving kids crazy is what parents are for right?* :)

She writes back: *guess so . . .*

He responds: *happy birthday!*

She responds: *thanks!*

And that, to her relief, is the end of the conversation. A few hours later her parents drive her to the train station. As always, her mother gives her a shoulder bag of leftovers that weighs more than her bag of clothes. She is halfway through the journey back when she remembers to open the envelope her father passed to her. Two fifty-euro bills, both so crisp they might be brand-new.

On Tuesday she takes the bus to the Appian Way Park. In the early days of Ayoub's absence, she came here often, making circuits through the park, feeling his presence like a finger about to tap on her shoulder, or a voice calling from just around the next bend of a tree-lined path. She didn't actually think he was there. But she couldn't deny that she felt something. When she described the experience to Sarah—maybe a year ago, in a phone call—she learned that it was, apparently, a common one. *I was said the exact thing by people in the situations which are similar to your situation. And I read about it in some articles and also some books.* Today is her first time back since that conversation. She imagines that Ayoub is back, walking next to her. She's telling him what it was like being here alone, feeling his presence. Afterward, they go for cappuccino at their favorite place. The owner is there, he remembers them—the cappuccino Arabs!—and asks where they've been, why he hasn't seen them for so long. Ayoub says he'll explain it all later. They sit and drink cappuccino and look into each other's eyes. She doesn't have to imagine him or not imagine him, remember him or not remember him, open his letters or not open his letters. Because he's just here. He's home.

"Can I ask you a question? About Ayoub?" That's what Paolo always says whenever he has a question about her husband. Usually he doesn't ask directly and instead waits for Amira to bring him up. Which she's grateful for. But she also likes that sometimes he just asks; it shows that he doesn't find the subject too radioactive to be acknowledged—that, to him, it's a part of life, and any part of life can be discussed.

"Ask away." They're sitting in a small square a short walk from his restaurant. He didn't bring any food today because she asked him not to: eating her mother's leftovers for two days has made her feel bloated. In fact, lying in bed the night before, she found herself worrying about the possibility that she would have to spend her meeting with Paolo straining to hold back her farts and, when she failed, worrying about whether he was smelling them.

"It might be a stupid question, though. Will you forgive me if it's stupid?"

"No promises."

"Why did you convert for him, and not him for you? I'm really just curious. Especially since he's not so observant."

The question takes her aback: she's told him, more than once, how sensitive she is to questions about her conversion. Her motivations. Whether she's a "real Muslim." She's told him how, sometimes, she's wished that Ayoub's own relationship to Islam was easier to define so that, by extension, hers would be too. She's told him that she knows in her heart her conversion was meaningful—of course it was!—

and she's told him how uncomfortable it makes her when people assume it's their right to attempt to pry that meaning from her.

She tries reminding herself he means no harm. She says something she thinks she's told him before: that she'd wanted to show Ayoub their marriage wasn't just him joining her life but also her joining his. "I think maybe part of it is that his parents were dead. Are dead. So Islam was this part of his life he could hold on to, and I could make that easier."

"When I heard about it, I thought it seemed very like you."

"Like me how?"

"Like how you always wanted something different from everyone else. To leave home, to live in Rome, to—"

"That's why I married my husband? To be different?"

"No, that's not what I'm saying."

"Well, what are you saying, then?"

"Just that when I heard, I wasn't surprised somehow. A lot of people aren't that open. But you are."

"It's not so different," she says. "One religion, another religion. People don't know what they're talking about." She feels that what she is saying is deeply true and important—and also that she sounds like an idiot.

"I'm sure you're right," he says. "Anyway, I still thought it was impressive, converting for someone. I don't know if I'm that open."

"Well, if you want to be open, you just do it. Just be open."

"You're probably right," he says.

Falling asleep in bed that night, she returns to the conversation and imagines flipping Paolo's questions around on him.

"Why are you a Catholic?" she asks him.

"Well—I just am."

"And you do every possible Catholic thing there is? Perform every ritual? Follow every principle? Build your life around them?"

"Probably not."

"So are you really a Catholic? Why not convert to some other religion?"

But even in her imagination, the questions don't work. Paolo just looks confused.

On another afternoon, maybe a week later, he asks about what she might be doing to push for Ayoub's release. Has she contacted the Ministry of Justice? What about the Italian embassy in Morocco? Is it possible to track down, or perhaps hire someone to track down, people with whom Ayoub was in contact in Pakistan, who could then testify to the true purpose of his visit? And what about his friend Arsalan? "If they were really just doing charity work—"

"What do you mean, 'if'?"

"No, nothing. Not—I didn't mean anything. I just meant, because he was just doing charity work—"

"If you meant 'because' and not 'if,' then why say 'if'?"

"I'm sorry," he says. "I was just trying to help. I just feel so bad."

She's mad for hours, but then the next day she's citing the conversation in an imaginary conversation with Meryem: *He's thinking of ways to help Ayoub!* Imaginary Meryem gives her a skeptical look that says, *That doesn't prove what you think it proves.*

The great virtue of an imaginary conversation is that you can always just declare it to be over.

On the phone her mother tries again to convince her to leave Esquilino. It's obvious that she's proud of herself for not having mentioned the subject for months—and obvious, too, that she thinks this has earned her a prize, and that the prize is her daughter moving. For a brief moment she is able to understand that her mother truly must feel compelled to say these things. (After all, it was not so long ago when she called to mention, in a serious tone, that she'd read about imams granting divorces to the wives of imprisoned men.) But this moment of empathy is quickly washed away by a wave of irritation.

"I'm not even saying move home, honey. I know you love Rome."

"Then what are you saying?"

"I'm saying—why Esquilino?"

"Because Esquilino is where Ayoub and I live. This is our home."

Is it really? The apartment—yes. But the neighborhood itself? She feels less at home there than she did when they moved in. It would be one thing if she were a stranger, an unknown. But instead she is, to so many people, *Ayoub's wife*. Whether anyone believes the accusations against him or not isn't what matters. What matters is that, for too many people, there is very little difference between the risk of association with a *terrorist* and the risk of association with an *accused terrorist*, little difference between *imprisoned* and *imprisoned without charge*. It might have been different if they'd lived in the neighborhood for longer before his absence; she might have forged more relationships. She might have real friends there besides Meryem. There might be some force in her life counterbalancing the heavy silence that presses down on her whenever she's in public. She might feel like slightly less of a liar, insisting to her mother that she doesn't want to move.

"Do you ever see any of your old girlfriends, at least? They were so sweet, those girls, especially—"

"They all dropped me, remember? My friends are here, in Esquilino. People are nice to me here."

The next time she and Paolo meet, neither of them mentions Ayoub, religion, or conversion. Instead, they talk about Paolo's roommates, who despite their foul housekeeping habits are growing on him. He still doesn't love sharing a room at thirty-two years old, but they're good people. They talk about rent, about how expensive Rome is compared to Avezzano, about the temptation he feels to move back home. Is it normal, he asks, to wonder all the time if he should be here? One of his roommates says it usually takes people a year to feel at home in the city. Is that normal? Is that how it was for her?

"I don't know what's 'normal,'" she says. "But no, it wasn't like that for me. I always knew I would stay."

Tuesday: walking. How many Romans have walked as many of the city's streets as she has? Not many, she guesses. In one sense this makes her a super-Roman; in another, she realizes, it makes her an outsider, because a true Roman feels at home in her corner of the city, wherever it is, and doesn't compulsively wander through other people's corners.

. . .

Sitting in a coffee bar, she surprises herself by ordering not just cappuccino but also a cannoli, telling herself she can afford it thanks to the hundred euros from her father. The word *cappuccino* brings a sneer to the waiter's face, and on Ayoub's behalf she welcomes it, not just the sneer itself but also her near certainty that the sneer is more pronounced because of her headscarf, that this is exactly how stupid this waiter is. It's the best cappuccino she's had in weeks. The cannoli's good too, but it's too much sugar, her body doesn't know what to do with it.

Back at home she crashes.

In the middle of the night she's up listening to screaming cats.

At Meryem's for tea, she says she's thinking about putting out some poison to stop the cats from coming around.

"Isn't that risky?" her friend asks. "I mean, maybe they're people's pets."

"I guess you're right," she says. "I'm just tired."

The next day she meets Paolo by the benches across from the Monti police station, an excellent spot for watching the neighborhood transitioning from day to night: different people on the streets, carrying themselves differently, dressing differently, different lighting, restaurant staff setting out boards advertising the evening's specials.

He's upset: a bad afternoon at work. He ruined a whole batch of pasta, and everyone saw, and then he was so upset that he misheard instructions for the soup, and then he ruined that, too.

"Did they have to throw it out?"

"No, thank God. The chef adapted it into something new on the spot."

"That's good."

"But he was furious. He said he had old friends coming tonight specifically for that soup."

"If he cared so much, he should have made it himself." This gets no response. "Anyway, things have been going well for you. This won't change that."

"You're right," he says. "You're right." They sit in silence—it's not awkward, it's perfectly comfortable—and then he says it again: yes, she's right, things are going well. So well, in fact, that he's finally decided to stay in Rome. He's speaking more slowly than usual, as if each word represents the next step down a path that, if he missteps, he will lose sight of and never be able to find again, and she realizes that until now she has failed to fully perceive that every time he talked about the question of staying or leaving, he really meant it: it wasn't just something to talk about; he was really working through the decision, which now, as a result, feels genuinely momentous. "You've helped me so much. I want you to know that. It's been hard, and you've really helped. You've really helped, Amira."

She should say something. If she doesn't say something, she'll cry. She has to start talking—start constructing, with words, a wall against tears. "Thank you."

"Thank *me*? I'm trying to thank *you*."

She shakes her head. "I know. But, I mean—thank you for saying so."

"You're thanking me for saying thank you?"

And then she's crying. She's sitting on a park bench with Paolo Orlandi, who once kissed her under the crisscrossing strands of lights in Camilla Russo's parents' backyard, who was the first person she made love with, in his older brother's friend's apartment, and she's sobbing. She's looking down and holding her eyes closed; she doesn't want anyone seeing her: the woman in the headscarf crying on the bench. The man with flour in his hair sitting awkwardly a full body's width away.

She feels a hand on her shoulder. Paolo is on her left, so the hand must be his right hand. His touch is light. More like the residue of a touch just withdrawn than an actual, ongoing touch.

"Sorry," he says softly. And then: "Is that okay?"

She doesn't look up or open her eyes or say anything.

The hand stays. And maybe her body becomes more accepting of the fact that it's there. And maybe the hand itself becomes less tentative, less poised to flee if not wanted. She's so unused to being touched that she can't tell the difference.

They go five days without any messages. She looks back over their old messages, counting how often it was him and how often it was her who wrote first to make plans. She tries to estimate—without getting too serious about it, without getting out pen and paper and actually making a tally—the average amount of time between their past meetings. Three days? Four? She admits to herself that she's worried he won't see her anymore. She can feel how much this would upset her: the exact weight of the blow, the shape and color of the bruise. Perhaps, she thinks, he is feeling something similar: perhaps he is digging through their old texts, worried that *she* is giving *him* the cold shoulder.

She tells herself it was nothing. A touch of comfort.

But then why isn't he messaging?

She goes to Meryem's for dinner, and because Meryem's husband is working late, she stays afterward to help bathe the children and put them to bed, a ritual in which pain and pleasure dance together so closely she can't pick them apart. She sits by the tub listening to Nada tell a story about her plastic bath toys: which of them are friends, which are fighting, how they've hurt each other's feelings but might reconcile soon. She mentally rehearses telling Meryem about Paolo. But no matter how she does it, no matter what she leaves out and what she includes, she dislikes the story. It doesn't sound like her life. It sounds like a cheap copy, distorted and unreal. She wishes she had shared the story earlier, when it was shorter and less complicated, when it was just a story about something that happened and not, inevitably, also a story about something she'd hidden. Nada holds her arms out, asking to be lifted from the tub. She's still light enough, just barely, to be lifted up by her armpits: a whole human moving through the air supported by Amira's two hands and nothing else.

After the children are in bed, she and Meryem sit on the couch drinking tea and talking quietly. She is halfway through her cup when her phone buzzes in her purse.

"Sorry," she says. "I should check that."

"Of course," says Meryem.

free after work tomorrow? :)

She decides the best thing to do is wait until she has left Meryem's apartment to respond. But her fingers are already typing.

yes. meet by the madonna fountain?

"Sorry," she says to Meryem. "This will just take a second."

"It's no problem."

sure, come hungry if you can :)

She puts her phone back in her purse.

"Good news?" says Meryem.

"What?"

"Something's got you smiling."

"Oh—no. I mean, yes. It's nothing. I mean—not nothing, but. It's my mother. She was waiting for some results. Medical tests. And apparently she got the results back today and it was all fine. I've been stressing about it all day, actually. I don't know why she took so long to tell me. I don't know why she waited until this late."

Meryem shrugs. "Who knows why our mothers do what they do?"

For the first time, he brings food that's not from his job: trapizzini from a place by the train stop. She recognizes the name on the cardboard box. She offers him money, which he refuses, and they find a bench where they can sit and eat together, talking like normal about their workdays, alternating who's talking and who's chewing and swallowing. When they're done eating, he takes the empty cardboard and their used napkins and tosses them in a nearby trash can.

"So," he says.

"So."

"So—this Saturday it's my birthday."

"Happy birthday! I had no idea."

"Well, I never said. Anyway—I'm having a party. Now that I'm staying, I should start acting like it. It won't be big—just my roommates, some people from the restaurant, maybe a cousin or two."

"Sounds fun."

"Will you come?"

"Me?"

"Yes, you. Of course."

She thinks about making up an excuse: she's going home again, or has to work, or already has another party to go to. But she wants to explain her real answer. She tries to tell him how difficult parties can be for her, the horrible itchiness of feeling that everyone may be watching her while pretending not to watch her, gathering data on her to use in conversation after she's gone. "I don't think I can explain how horrible it is. You have to just trust me. I'm—"

"I trust you," he says. "I believe you. But listen. No one at the party knows anything about you."

"No?"

"No."

"You haven't told your roommates about me? About Ayoub?"

"Of course not."

"Why not?"

"I don't know. Because it's not my place. And anyway—"

"I'd have my headscarf on."

"Well, yes, I assumed so. But you can say whatever you like about yourself to people. Or not say. Will you come? Please?" He clasps his hands together and sticks out his bottom lip like an imploring child, and for a moment she can see it— can imagine herself at a party where whatever people know about her, they know it only because she's told them.

"Okay. I'll come."

Paolo bolts up and pumps his arm. "Yes! Yes!" The arm pumping turns into an improvised little shimmy dance. "This is good! This is great!" Two teenage girls walking by glance at each other and smile and start walking faster, trying to get away before the urge to laugh overtakes them.

Her phone starts buzzing from her purse. "Hold on," she says. "Let me check this."

SARAH LAWYER OFFICE.

This time, she knows, it cannot be a wrong number. Sarah—careful Sarah, conscientious Sarah—wouldn't make the same mistake twice. No. She knows, just knows, she's about to get bad news, news that can't wait, the worst news.

"Who is it?" says Paolo. "What is it, Amira?"

Ayoub is dead.

Sarah doesn't know anything else yet.

Doesn't know how he died, just that he's dead, Amira will never see him alive again.

No one will ever see Ayoub alive again.

Images of the future form and disintegrate in her mind's eye: packing up the apartment, loading things into her parents' car, moving back to Avezzano, back into her old room.

She sees herself sitting at her parents' dining room, eating, they're sad for her but also relieved, it's like she never left, it was all a dream.

Ayoub is dead.

Amira hasn't even answered the phone yet, and she's sure of it.

"Hello?" The worst news is descending on her at high speed, a bomb dropped from the sky and programmed to seek out her and only her, to smash into her and rip itself apart and rip her apart with it. She's living now in the moment right before she's ripped apart. The phone in her hand. The residue of trapizzini grease on and around her lips in the spots that she missed with her napkin. Paolo looking at her with intent concern. The pair of giggling teenage girls breaking into full-throated laughter because they can't help it. When Sarah does speak—"He is going home!"—she doesn't understand, in part because Sarah's Italian always takes her an extra second to understand, but more because what she's saying—"He is going home!"—is an idea that, no matter how many times she has imagined it, now turns out to be beyond her ability to understand.

Paolo has no idea what's happening. He's trying to catch her eye and waiting for her to say something, anything.

And Sarah just keeps saying the unbelievable thing: "He is going home, Amira! He is going home!"

For the first time since the week when Ayoub went missing, she calls in sick to work. For the first time in so long—for the first time ever, she feels—she makes a shopping list. For the first time in so long, she goes to the market with the big rolling grocery cart, shopping for more than the cheapest ingredients for the simplest stew. She picks out vegetables and herbs, couscous and rice and pasta, lentils and flour, chicken and lamb, mozzarella and Parmesan and cream and eggs: everything she needs for his favorite Moroccan dishes and everything she needs for his favorite Italian dishes and everything she needs for tonnarelli alla Ayoub, which she started making for him just a few months into their marriage, after she saw it in a dream, tonnarelli with chicken harira—extra thick, the way he'd taught her to make it, the way his mother had made it when he was a child—ladled on top.

When she sees Walid moving through the aisles of the market, surveying his neighbors' offerings, she can't resist heading toward him.

They exchange salaams and he peers into her cart. "A lot of food today," he says in Italian.

"Yes," she says in Arabic. "It is."

"Are you expecting guests?" He peeks into the cart again, like he thinks a second look will help him deduce the answer.

She follows his gaze into her cart, as if considering for the first time that its contents might require an explanation. "Oh, no. No guests. It's just that Ayoub will be home on Sunday." Somehow, out of everyone, Walid is the first person she has told. Not her parents, not Mourad in Madrid, not Meryem. She's been holding the news inside, asserting her authority—her right—to savor it privately. To know something about herself that no one else knows.

"Really?" he says. It's beautiful, watching the surprise reconfigure his face.

"Yes."

"Well . . . that's wonderful news, isn't it? He was found innocent, then? Cleared?"

"Well, he was never charged with anything, so there was never anything to be found innocent of. There were no charges. Remember?"

"I see. Well. How odd."

Walking home, she wonders how quickly the news will spread: which person Walid will tell first, and how soon, and the exact words he will use, and what that person's face will look like. Maybe he's told someone already. Maybe that person has told someone else. Maybe they're telling someone else right now.

Sarah warns her not to throw a party. "I've seen it be a badness too many times," she says. That's fine: she doesn't need to throw a party. She just wants to cook all of Ayoub's dishes, wants her husband's favorite foods ready for him when he gets home. For the first time in over two years, she gets out her pots, pans, baking sheets, spices. She calls Meryem and they cry together on the phone, then Meryem comes over with Nada. For the first time in over two years, the apartment fills up with true cooking smells. They chop and cut and mix and bake and boil and simmer. They make up jobs for Nada: Get this from the pantry, get that, wipe out this bowl please, taste this. She teaches Meryem and Nada "Cooking in the Afternoon," a song from her childhood:

Cooking in the afternoon
Cooking while the sun's still up
Tonight's meal is just a dream
But I am the cook
The cook who dreams
And makes the dreams come true

They sing together—their voices interacting with each other and with the gurgles of the simmering food, the whir of the oven fan, the ticking of two different timers (one counting down for the lamb, one for the chicken). When was the last time she sang?

"Can I show you something?" she says.

"Of course," says Meryem.

She goes to the spare room and takes down the shoebox of letters. Back in the kitchen, she sets the box on the table and gestures for Meryem to sit.

Once she's settled in, Meryem lifts the top off. "Are these ... ?"

Amira nods. She sees the fear in her friend's eyes. "You don't have to," she says. "But if you want. Or later. I didn't mean to put you on the spot."

"No," says Meryem. "I want to. I mean, if you want me to."

Watching Meryem read, she breathes through her mouth to avoid smelling the Temara smell that may or may not be there. She watches Meryem's eyes move from the letters to Nada, who is drawing with crayon and paper on the floor in the hallway, then back to the letters, then back to Nada, then back to the letters.

She leaves Meryem with the letters and walks to the living room. Sitting on the couch, she takes out her phone and texts Paolo: *I need to give all my energy to my family right now,*

I hope you understand. Thank you for everything. Please don't contact me or come by the store, it's too complicated. I hope you have a good birthday. She goes through and deletes every text he sent to her, every text she sent to him. She deletes him from her address book. It was just yesterday that they said goodbye in front of the fountain, but already it feels like a lifetime ago.

When she goes back to the kitchen, Meryem is closing the shoebox. "Thank you," she says. "Thank you for sharing that with me. You hear about these things. Stories. I remember, growing up—it's different, I know. But—well. Thank you."

Before Meryem leaves to get her own family's dinner started, she asks Amira if she wants to pray. They've prayed together before, but this time feels different: less like a daily ritual and more like a ceremony marking a whole new stage of life, like a wedding or a funeral. As they lower their heads to the floor, Amira begins to cry—silently at first, but then louder, and with a force that undoes her ability to form words. After the second rak'ah, Meryem stops. Amira thinks that her friend is waiting for her to gather herself so they can proceed together. But then she realizes that Meryem is sobbing too.

"What's wrong, Mommy?" says Nada, who has not yet memorized the prayers and so has been off to the side, imitating her way along. "Why are you crying?"

"What did you say, sweetie?" Meryem asks, buying herself a second to wipe her face on her sleeve.

"I said, why are you crying? What's wrong?"

"Because, sweetie, Amira's husband is coming home. Ayoub."

"Amira's married?"

"Yes, Nada. Remember? I told you."

"Where is he?"

"Back in Morocco, sweet one."

"Morocco where you came from?"

"Yes."

"Why?"

"It's hard to explain, darling. I'll have to tell you later."

"Why are you crying?"

"Because I'm happy. Sometimes we cry when something good is happening."

"Why is Amira crying?"

"I told you, sweetie. Because she's happy. Ayoub's coming home, and she's very, very happy."

BRADLEY

The idea for the prank came to him on a Friday afternoon. He was sitting in a booth at Genova's, eating a turkey-and-bacon sandwich, working through a real estate catalog he'd picked up at Speedway on Tuesday and had ever since been saving for a moment exactly like this one. To eat a Genova's turkey-and-bacon sandwich while flipping, pen in hand, through a real estate catalog was one of life's great uncomplicated pleasures. Extra pickle, extra onion, a regular amount of yellow mustard. Did he actually, on this particular Friday afternoon, want to buy a new house? Probably not. He loved his home, loved the million little modifications and upgrades he and Sheri had made over the years, inching it ever closer to perfection. But it was fun to shop: shopping proved that staying put wasn't inertia but a choice, one he was making again and again.

Once a month or so, if he saw a particularly interesting listing—and if work wasn't too busy—he set up a showing. Sheri didn't approve. "The poor agents," she said. "Aren't you just wasting their time?" Sheri was sweet. Wonderfully sweet. But in this case he suspected his wife had it wrong. After an agent showed him a house, that agent could then turn around and say to every other potential buyer: *I actually showed this house to Bradley Welk just the other day.* Or: *I was showing Bradley Welk some properties last week, and he said . . .*

He wasn't conceited, he told himself. He just knew how people thought. If a prominent person wanted something, then an average person was more likely to want it too. If a prominent person sought the advice of a particular real estate agent, then an average person was likely to do the same. This wasn't a good thing or a bad thing: it was just the way it was. Anyway, if you were a real estate agent, then showing people houses was your job. If you didn't like your job, you could get another one.

Genova's made the best deli sandwiches in Springwater. No competition. It was the rolls: they baked their own, every morning. There was no point going anywhere else.

The first house in the catalog that caught his eye was out in Benson. The house itself didn't look particularly special—and he would never live so far from town—but it had dormer windows on the second floor, and he'd loved dormer windows for as long as he could remember, even as a child watching the world go by from the back seat of his parents' teal Pontiac. Better yet, it had a pool. For years, he'd been thinking of having a pool dug in the backyard; maybe, he thought, looking at someone else's pool—an actual pool, not a picture in a catalog—would help put the decision in motion. He circled the listing.

When he reached the end of the catalog, his sandwich was done and he'd circled another half-dozen houses. Seven total. He reviewed his picks, trying to eliminate all but the best two. Only then did he notice that the selling agent for the house with the dormer windows and pool was Melanie. "Wow," he said aloud. As far as he knew—and he was reasonably confident that his knowledge was up to date—this house was bigger and more expensive than Melanie's usual stock. A step up the real estate ladder. Years ago, he remembered, she'd worked right here, in Genova's, ringing up orders behind the cash register. Now she was selling—or at least trying to sell—nice big houses with dormer windows and pools. "Good for her," he murmured. "Good. For. Her."

He recircled the listing—had he not seen her name there, he likely would have crossed it out—and the first tendrils of the idea for the prank started pushing upward into his conscious mind. Already, he could see the smile it would bring to Melanie's face. She had a good smile, the kind that didn't just show you she was happy but also, through a force of its own, lifted her up to a higher plane of happiness, right there in front of you. He'd always loved her smile.

Back at the office, he tore the listing from the catalog, handed it to his secretary, and told her to call and set up a showing ("Make sure it's with Melanie Kinston") for next Thursday or Friday afternoon. "Don't use my real name."

"Why not?" She made a face like he'd ordered her to prank call a cancer ward.

"Because I'm a private person." *And because I'm your boss and I said so,* he added silently.

Driving home from work, he debated how to spend his night. Sheri was in Fayetteville, helping her mother recover from knee replacement surgery. He'd made omelets three nights in a row. He was proud of his omelet-making skills, but the idea of another omelet—home alone on a Friday night, watching whatever on TV—depressed him.

At the Speedway he sat in his truck by the pump and called his son, Paul, who didn't answer, probably because he was heading to dinner with friends, or already eating dinner with friends, or hanging out with friends after an early dinner, getting ready for a night out. Jealousy came lunging, and he wasn't fast enough to stop it from stabbing him in the chest. To be a college freshman on a Friday night! Rubbing up close against possibility, raw and endless, or at least endless feeling, which was just about as good. To spend an evening with Paul! If Paul was home, they could get barbecue and watch whatever on TV and it wouldn't be depressing. It would be wonderful. It would be the most wonderful thing in the world.

It was only when he got out of the truck and started pumping gas that he noticed Melanie was at the pump across from his, filling up her gray Civic. He considered himself a relatively nonsuperstitious person. However, he did sometimes have the sense that an invisible network of wires connected everything and everyone, transferring energy back and forth between desires and outcomes, calling the world into being, keeping it in motion.

Melanie's son, Michael, was also a freshman in college. Also an only child. Watching her pump gas, he wondered if she, too, was thinking about her son, wishing he were home tonight. He had been grateful, for the last few weeks, that Michael was gone. All summer the boy had worked the Genova's cash register, saving money for school. Which was a fine thing to do, of course—and it must have been fun for him and his mother to compare notes—but he hated running into the kid on his lunch breaks. The first Monday that Michael hadn't been there, he'd been relieved, and now the memory of that relief felt a little guilty. Of course Melanie missed her son—just as much as he missed Paul.

"Melanie!" As far as he knew, he was the only person who didn't call her Mel. It started innocently, or at least unconsciously. Only over time did it become a low-risk way for him to acknowledge their secret in public. *Melanie,* he could say, and in his mouth it was sneakily intimate, while to anyone listening—besides her—it was just a name.

She startled, saw him, smiled. Maybe blushed a little; the massive bank of fluorescent lights overhead made it hard to tell. She looked tired, but this, too, might have been the harsh lights more than anything else. They talked easily, like they always had, long before anything happened between them. She told him about a house she'd shown that afternoon, one she'd been showing for months. People kept wanting to see it, but no one ever wanted to buy, and she couldn't figure out why ("They don't seem to know why themselves"). It used to be an interesting puzzle, but now it was just irritating. Other people at the gas station could see them talking, but that was fine. People were allowed to talk. Everyone knew they sat on the school board together. They were allowed to be friendly.

He told her about his dinner dilemma. "I miss Paul," he said, and it felt good to say something simple and true.

"I miss Michael," she said. He wondered what it was like for her and Art: if, like him and Sheri, they were reckoning with not just the absence of their child but also whatever that absence revealed, the way removing the furniture and rugs from a house made it impossible to ignore your dust creatures and scuff marks, everything you had at some point dropped on the floor and forgotten about, or hadn't even realized you'd dropped in the first place.

Melanie's pump clicked.

A few seconds later, his did the same.

"Do you want to come over for dinner?" she said.

He'd already opened his mouth to turn her down when she added that Art was out of town, at a work conference. "Nothing fancy. Probably a frozen casserole."

"I don't know, Melanie. Sounds cold."

On the way he stopped for a bottle of wine, something he thought he remembered she liked. A familiar bouncy song came on the radio, and he drummed along on the steering wheel. Desire and outcome. Just a few hours ago he'd circled Melanie's name in the catalog, and now he was headed to her house. Calling the world into being.

He knew that nine out of ten outside observers would say they were *having an affair*. But he'd always rejected that phrase. Ditto for *cheating*. The terms might have been technically accurate, but in practice they seemed hopelessly obtuse. Calling what he had with Melanie *an affair* was like calling a house *an assemblage of wood and various other materials*. Right—but wrong. What they had was a string of moments like this one. Improvised. Little or no talk about what they were doing, what they'd done, what it meant, or might mean, or should mean. No talk about Sheri, about Art. Nothing about mortgages, tuition, retirement, business up, business down. Each time was an independent event: they never made plans for the next time, or even verified that there would be a next time. For months, everything would go back to normal. And then it would happen again. Each time had the surprise and unpredictability of a first, or an isolated one-off. But also: each time they knew each other better, were better together. They had fun. He continued to be a good husband to Sheri. *Affairs* hurt people; *cheating* ruined lives. This was something else.

As he approached her driveway, he saw a car coming toward him on the other side of the road. Just in case, he drove an extra mile down the road then turned around. He told himself his turn signal hadn't been on at Melanie's house; no one in the other car could have guessed where he'd been headed.

When he pulled up in front of her garage, the good bouncy song was still playing, so he kept the truck on until it finished, letting his anticipation build.

The front door was open; he shut and locked it behind him. Headed to the kitchen. He'd been here before—before anything happened—to work on school board business. It wasn't a house where he could ever live, at least not in its current state. He was too attached to new construction, flat and flush surfaces, new paint, new finishes and fixtures. But tonight the house was just right: a portal to another life, or at least to forgetting about his own. As far as he knew, he liked his life. But that didn't make slipping out of it for a few hours any less fun.

In the kitchen she was facing away from him, fiddling with the oven. He set the wine on the table and stood just behind her, as close as possible without their bodies touching. Put his hand to the back of her neck, felt her wanting his touch, knowing nine-tenths of the way exactly how good it would feel but desperate for the last tenth, for confirmation, the merging of fantasy and reality. They braced together against the oven, removing and reconfiguring their clothes only to the minimum extent required, their wedding rings at one point slipping and jamming against each other. Then they moved upstairs and took off their clothes and did it again on the hallway carpet. Everything just happened. This was the exact quality he most missed during sex with Sheri: things just happening. But he wasn't thinking about that now, which was the point, he was in the moment. Melanie cried out so loudly he worried, however irrationally, that someone might hear. Reflexively, he put a hand to her mouth—not hard, there was no possibility of stopping her from breathing. She bit down—not hard, she didn't break the skin, but it was definitely a bite—and the pain became pleasure and the pleasure ran through him like wind running through blades of grass and he brayed like a farm animal and for as long as it lasted didn't care who heard.

He didn't know what it was about her that made him so energetic. Like a teenager. She wasn't his type—at all. Years ago, when he first saw her at Genova's, her looks did nothing for him. And it wasn't like she'd changed much since then. Certainly very few people would rate her as high as Sheri, he was sure of that.

When they were done in the hallway, she led him to the bedroom, where they fell together on the bed in comfortable spent silence.

A loud electronic chime came from downstairs. He bolted up, sure it was the doorbell, that he was caught; even if he could hide, his truck was right outside. He'd been a fool, he saw now, a complete fool, putting his whole life in the balance—for what? A few minutes of fun. Lust. The chime came again, and in the chiming he heard a horrible truth about himself: that he didn't know what he was doing, didn't understand life or his place in it, did too many things just to prove that he could.

Melanie smiled. Her good smile: happy and making herself happier. "It's the oven. The casserole's ready."

He fell back onto the bed and pressed toward her, but she twisted away, saying it would be sad to have remembered to set the timer, then let the house burn down anyway.

When she came back, she had a tray with two plates of casserole and two glasses of wine. The casserole was fantastic: taco fixings mixed with curly corkscrew pasta. "Is it beef?"

She shook her head. "Turkey." She was smiling even bigger now. "You want the recipe?"

Heading down Melanie's stairs for water from Melanie's kitchen faucet, he thought about alternate universes. A month ago he'd read an article, in a magazine at his dentist's office, about the likely proliferation of multiple existences, all smudged and fractured versions of each other. In one universe, maybe, *Art* was walking naked down the stairs at *his* house. Having just had sex with Sheri three times. One of Sheri's casseroles digesting inside him.

Could it be wrong to feel this good? If it was a matter of just stray moments here and there being put to use for pleasure, and no one ever found out? He loved Sheri no less, was depriving her of nothing. In fact, he could see how there might be an argument that what had happened between him and Melanie was good for his marriage. Just a few days ago, he'd managed to tell Sheri that he wished she would sometimes be the one to initiate their lovemaking. That he needed to know she wanted him. The conversation had been awkward—but, he thought, good in the end. Would he ever have found the motivation to plunge into that awkwardness without his experiences with Melanie? He could imagine how horrible the question would sound to another person—let alone Sheri—but that didn't mean there was no truth to it.

In the kitchen, the first thing he saw was Michael, standing by the sink with his arms crossed.

In the days that followed he would spend a great deal of mental energy on pointless questions. How did they not hear a car pull up? How did they not hear the front door open? How did they not hear that someone was moving around downstairs? Exactly when did Michael come in, and exactly what did he hear? What was he thinking, standing there by the sink? How long would he have stood there waiting if no one had come downstairs?

But for now these questions were in the future. Now he was standing there naked and wondering what to do: what to do in general and what to do right away with his naked body.

He put both hands over his crotch.

"Don't say anything," Michael hissed.

He nodded.

"I knew it was you." The boy took a step forward, and for a second Bradley thought he was about to get spat on. He tried to think of something to say. He heard Melanie's steps on the stairs; from the look on Michael's face, he thought that if only he could stop time, he could convince the boy to leave before it was too late.

But it was already too late.

For all the times he'd heard the phrase *the color left her face,* he'd never actually seen the color draining from someone's face in real time. Until now. Thankfully, Melanie wasn't naked; she'd put on a purple robe he'd never seen before. *The color left her face.* It was nauseating.

"Jesus," said Michael. "Jesus Christ. Fuck this. Fuck. This." On the way to the door he kicked at a chair, obviously hoping it would crash to the floor, or at least smash into the table. But the kick didn't really connect, and the chair barely wobbled. "Fuck this!"

The door slammed. Then came a high-pitched scraping sound that, in the moment, Bradley couldn't identify, but that he would soon realize was one of Michael's keys running hard against the driver's side door of his truck. He would tell Sheri it happened while he was at Genova's, and she would be horrified that something like that could happen in Springwater.

MEL

They met in the library. After a few whispered conversations about the papers they were writing, Art asked her out. Their first date was supposed to be *The Killing Fields* and dinner. But on the afternoon of the agreed-upon day, he called to say that the university endowment board had just voted to continue investing its funds in South African companies. There was a sit-in happening at the chancellor's office, and probably a march afterward. Could they do the movie next time?

She followed his directions to the imitation South African shantytown the protesters had built outside the chancellor's office, and arrived just in time to join the march. It was obvious that Art knew people there. Until then, her own knowledge of protests was almost entirely secondhand: newspapers, magazines, TV, movies. Especially movies, which was probably why walking down Franklin Street with Art felt movie-like, every second part of an unfolding, accumulating story that their presence was revealing, to themselves and everyone watching, their bodies combining with all the other bodies to stop anything else from occupying the street other than their demand, which was suddenly Mel's demand, too: *DIVEST!* It was magic, and the magic was still there in the morning when she woke up in Art's bed. He started taking her to speeches, panels, documentary screenings, more marches, sit-ins, letter-writing sessions, strategy debates. Apartheid. CIA meddling in South America. Nuclear proliferation. She was twenty-one. He was twenty-five, a grad student. They never saw *The Killing Fields*.

They moved together to a small wooden house on Carlson Street. The day after they moved in, Mel was unpacking when the doorbell rang. And that was how she met Linda, who was standing on her front stoop, smiling as if she already knew they would become best friends, holding a pie tin covered in aluminum foil and a brochure: "The Top Dangerous Myths of the Nuclear Lobby."

Linda and her husband, Robert, lived just four doors down, in a small wooden house that was almost identical to theirs. That night, the four of them sat on Linda and Robert's screened-in porch—which was the same as their screened-in porch, but with a table and chairs—eating fish tacos and drinking and talking past midnight about politics, activism, school, childhood, what they were reading, what they were learning. At least once a week for the next two years, they did it again: stayed up late sliding effortlessly from the immediate (whether so-and-so had procured the correct permit for an upcoming march) to the grand (the future they were hoping to use the march to call into being) and back again (immediate) and again (grand). Did marches work? What would this particular march actually accomplish? Should they order pizza? Who had to be up early tomorrow? Who was ready for another beer? Dinner was never just dinner, going for a walk wasn't just going for a walk. Everything was bigger. Everything connected.

Later, when she looked back on this time of her life, what Mel remembered most was a certain easy intimacy. They stopped by each other's houses just to see who was home.

They went grocery shopping together, cooked together, ate together, marched together, locked arms on Franklin Street. They invited people over to show off what they had, the friendship they'd found. Hugging Linda and Robert goodbye at the end of an evening they'd spent together, she often felt sure not only that she and Art were going to make love once they were alone but also that Linda and Robert were, too, and that all four of them knew it but didn't need to say anything. She and Art got married in Linda and Robert's backyard, with Robert officiating, giving a beautiful speech about *loving in history*. She'd never been so happy, and never known for sure that happiness like this was actually possible for grown-ups.

Art was finishing a graduate degree in social work, tutoring undergrad psychology majors for money. Mel was halfway through a history major and working at a health food store. Robert had just started a doctorate in history. Linda was finishing a political science major and working at a garden supply center, always bringing home seeds and clippings and plants for their little yards. Mel sometimes suspected that either Linda or Robert had some other source of money at their disposal—but she never knew for sure.

She understood that they would leave Carlson Street someday, but she couldn't imagine why, or when. Then Art finished his degree and struggled to find a job that put it to use. He tutored more, but found tutoring increasingly unbearable now that he was officially qualified for something else. In private, he complained to her that everyone but him was still on some kind of track. His interest in activism swung back and forth. Sometimes he seemed done with it, as if, without knowing where his own life was headed, he couldn't marshal the energy to be interested in where the rest of the world was going. At other times, he seemed like more of an activist than any of them, as if he were channeling the energy he wasn't able to pour into his career. His demeanor at protests changed, and he began—in Mel's eyes, anyway—to resemble just slightly the people, mostly men, who showed up primarily so they could engineer antagonistic confrontations with the police. She worried, but not terribly. Everything would be normal again, she felt, as soon as he found work.

How would their life have been different if the state health department had not decided to open a new public health clinic in Springwater, serving all of Yew County?

If, when looking for the clinic's first employees, the state hadn't written to Professor William Townsend of the University of North Carolina School of Social Work, urging him to solicit applications from his most promising recent graduates?

If Art had never taken any of Townsend's classes?

If he'd been offered any other job in his field?

If, in December 1985, a few weeks before her graduation, Mel had not found out she was pregnant?

At first they thought Art might commute. But the drive was an hour each way, which meant two hours away from the baby. Plus gas money. Plus paying Durham rent on a Springwater salary.

Linda took the news hard. It was as if, to her, their decision to leave Durham amounted to a judgment that nothing had ever been good there. Every time they got together, she retold the story of the one time she and Robert went to Yew County, for a counterprotest against a KKK rally in Springwater. On the drive they passed a sign by the side of the highway: WELCOME TO KLAN COUNTRY. It was rusted and full of holes—but it was there. "We couldn't believe it, could we?" she said. "Klan Country! In 1984!" The rally itself, at least in Linda's telling, was even more shocking. She and Robert had been prepared, she said, for the white hoods. What they hadn't known to expect was all the people who showed up wearing normal weekend clothes, no hoods or masks at all. "On the Klan side! These are your new neighbors."

They promised they wouldn't be gone long. They would keep looking for jobs "back here." Something would come up. In the meantime, an hour wasn't far. They could visit on weekends.

"That's what everyone says," said Linda. "That's what everyone says when they move away."

The first time Robert and Linda came to visit Springwater, they'd barely walked in the door when Linda said, "I can't believe it—that Klan sign is still there!"

Which, yes, it was. They were aware. Of course they were aware.

But why did it have to be the very first thing out of Linda's mouth?

When she went to the bathroom, Robert quietly apologized. "She's just hurting. She misses you. We both do."

The house they'd rented in Springwater was spacious but uncomfortable: dusty in a way that no amount of dusting would ever address. Without Durham's steady stream of students and visiting professors, the rental market had less to offer; it made more sense to buy, especially with a child. So they bought, telling themselves that buying didn't mean they had to stay. But their inspector failed to detect the sinkhole in the yard, let alone the fact that it was growing, threatening to swallow the house. There was a solution, which like many solutions could be summarized by a single word: *money*. Art got more clinical training. Got promoted. Got a raise. Once Michael started school, Mel started working again, first at

Genova's, because that was all she could find. She got a real estate license, toughed it through the early years of getting her name out, learning the market. After that, moving would have meant starting over. They fixed the sinkhole. They started paying off the house faster. The house gained value. Michael grew up and made friends and didn't miss Carlson Street, for the simple reason that he'd never lived there. Back in Durham, Robert became a professor. Linda went into business as a "nonprofit consultant." Neither Mel nor Art was able to figure out if she actually made any money.

For a while, whenever they saw each other, Linda would at some point compulsively run through the news of every group and cause they were involved with or thinking about becoming involved with. Sometimes these updates felt like an accusation: *Here's something good you're not doing, and here's another, and here's another, you've changed, you said you'd come back and you didn't, and you won't, because you've changed, and not for the better.* Over time, the updates came less frequently. Then they stopped. When they saw each other, they didn't talk about activism anymore, and didn't talk about not talking about activism, either. Instead: Michael, their jobs, home improvement projects, vacations, the various approaches to exercise and food and sleep they were trying on their aging bodies. They were, it turned out, still capable of closeness. Maybe not the daily same-street intimacy of before, but something Mel felt sure could be just as deep. Linda and Robert loved Michael, and showered him with presents. He saw them as an aunt and uncle. In a fireproof safe in the back of their bedroom closet, and also in their lawyer's office in downtown Springwater, there was a document establishing that if she and Art both died and Michael still required a legal guardian, he would go and live with them.

When, after many attempts, Robert and Linda decided to stop actively trying to get pregnant, and not to adopt, Mel and Art were the first people they told. They sat together in Linda and Robert's living room—not on Carlson Street, they'd moved long ago—and all cried together, even Art, who never cried, and while of course Mel was unhappy that her friends were in pain, she was grateful to know they could all still sit and feel intensely together.

In the spring of 2001, Mel sold a house to a woman named Sheila Pacon, a longtime member of the local school board. A few weeks later, Sheila called to ask Mel if she would consider running for a board seat that fall. Officially, the board was nonpartisan: you ran as yourself, not as a Democrat or a Republican. But increasingly, Sheila said, everyone knew who was who, and board disputes broke down along party lines; she was recruiting Democrats with the energy to stand up to the Republican bloc and make it official that not everyone in Springwater worshipped George W. Bush. Mel didn't run to impress Linda and Robert, but she did hope they would be impressed—that they might see her campaign as a direct extension of all their old conversations about how to nudge the world in the right direction. (They had, over time, shown a willingness to see Art's work in this light.) She even hoped they might join her campaign, helping to design flyers and corral volunteers and knock on doors. But when she brought it up, she sensed that Linda was uninterested and that her lack of interest was motivated by a need, perhaps unconscious, to punish her. *You abandoned us, now we abandon you,* though of course, Linda never said that, or anything like it. When she won, her old boss at Genova's, a man named Sam who normally did nothing without weeks of planning, was so proud that he threw her an impromptu victory party. Sandwiches on the house. She invited Linda and Robert. They didn't come.

Serving on the school board was rewarding. She talked more to her fellow parents, worked to understand their perspectives, spent time learning how they thought. Selling houses had made her better at talking, and much better at listening. Too many of the other board members saw their job as to cut as much as possible: cut classes, cut activity budgets, cut teacher protections. She hated it. But she knew they were cutting less, and more carefully, thanks to resistance from her and Sheila and whoever else they were able to recruit case by case. From either party. It wasn't glamorous. She had very few obvious victories to point to. But she never doubted that the work mattered.

She was just over a year into her first term when Linda called to invite her and Art to a protest in Durham against the imminent invasion of Iraq. The call was strange. Linda gave no preamble—no introductory acknowledgment that she was about to launch into a conversation of a type they'd stopped having long ago. It was as if, in her mind, they had already spent the morning discussing not just Iraq but this particular protest, when in fact they had never discussed either. "I think we can do it, Melly. I really think we can. We just need to push. We need to push and push and push." She sounded like she was about to cry.

Neither Mel nor Art ended up attending the protest—or any Iraq protest. At least once a week, Mel got a new "IRAQ ACTION BLAST" email stuffed with details about meetings and protests Linda hoped people would attend, congressional offices Linda hoped people would call, links to articles Linda hoped people would read and forward to their friends and family. Articles about the complete lack of a Saddam–9/11 connection. Reports on how the CIA had been pressured to fake the necessary facts. Investigations chronicling the Bush family's long-running and transparently pathological fixation on Saddam. Spiderweb diagrams that promised to illuminate exactly how Dick Cheney, his family, and their nefarious associates stood to profit from invasion. Mel sometimes skimmed these emails and sometimes deleted them without reading and sometimes let them languish unread in her inbox. Art did the same. They never went to a single meeting, made a single phone call, gave any money. It wasn't that they *supported* the war. Of course not. They were just . . . doing other things. Mel knew this explanation sounded pathetic, even when uttered only silently, to herself. At the same time, she felt strongly that this was the exact definition of adult life: selecting, from a near infinity of choices, to do some things and not others, knowing at every turn that you could be choosing differently, and that it was impossible to know for sure you were making the right choice. She did wonder, later, about the extent to which her cool response to Linda's invitation was influenced by her old friend's non-reaction to her school board run. But she didn't think it was possible to know.

The rest of 2003, they hardly saw each other at all. Again, it wasn't something they ever talked about or made official. It was just a cooling, one that, most days, Mel hardly noticed or thought about. Michael started his junior year of high school and began researching colleges. Art got another promotion, becoming less of a full-time therapist and more of an administrator. She wasn't sure it was a good idea: she couldn't see him enjoying himself with drastically less one-on-one patient contact. He went to work earlier in the morning; he made more money.

In the fall of 2004, two more Democrats got elected to the board, and three Republicans retired, two of them replaced by fellow Republicans with even more interest in cuts and even less interest in compromise. Negotiations over the following year's budget became so heated that it was decided that two board members—one Republican and one Democrat—should meet on their own, without the others, to hash out the general contours of an agreement. Nothing binding, but something they could all look at together and debate, rather than just yelling at each other. The Democrats picked Mel—they would have picked Sheila, out of deference to her seniority, but Sheila herself admitted that she wasn't sure she could keep her cool—and the Republicans picked Bradley Welk, a local lawyer new to the board. Mel knew about him only what everyone in Springwater knew: that he had an office downtown, just off the courthouse square; that he could often be seen walking between his office and the courthouse; that he wore khakis and blue button-down shirts; that he played golf; that he had a son, Paul, who was Michael's age; that he wore aviator sunglasses with silver frames; that his truck was always shiny and spotless; that his father, a prominent local Republican, had died over the summer. "Good luck," said Sheila. "That's all I can say—good luck."

She had never cheated on Art and had never considered cheating on Art. Not with any degree of seriousness. Because it had crossed her mind so rarely, she'd never given much thought to why people had sex with people other than their spouses. Perhaps this is why, when she first slept with Bradley, she felt so unequipped to understand what was happening. In his office, of all places. They'd been discussing the possible responses of their fellow board members to their proposed budget compromise, and they were trading imitations back and forth—Bradley was pretending to be Norman Lightfield, who always used both hands for handshakes, no matter who he was talking to—and laughing and laughing, and then they were on his desk. Afterward, she didn't think it would happen again. She told herself that the thrill had something to do with verifying that life was never fixed, that surprise was always possible—and that this type of thing didn't have to be verified often to know it was true. Everyone was happy, or happy enough, with the budget draft they came up with; board meetings got less heated. A month passed, and this month seemed like proof that what happened on Bradley's desk had really been a one-time thing. Then it happened again. Not on the desk, but she felt sure she loved Art no less. She couldn't believe how smooth Bradley's skin was, and couldn't believe the way its smoothness unlatched some trapdoor she'd never noticed right beneath her, how she fell through, faster every second. She'd never really thought about the smoothness of a man's skin before. The only person she could imagine bringing it up with was Linda, but she never did.

Every time, she thought she and Bradley were done; every time, they weren't. She tried to avoid thinking about what it meant, because whenever she did, she ended up feeling horrible.

She read online about breakfasts: about how, if a school district made free or reduced-cost breakfasts available to its students, the federal government would pick up half the cost. She read studies about the impact of going without breakfast on children's ability to learn. She looked up statistics about food insecurity and chronic hunger in North Carolina and, to the extent they were available, in Yew County specifically.

She read about failure rates, repeat rates, dropout rates, the cost of summer school, the costs of an undereducated population. She spent an afternoon at a cabin on Angleton Lake with Bradley, drifting between sex, her argument on behalf of a countywide breakfast program, his devil's advocate counterargument, and, eventually, joint strategizing about how to sell it to the rest of the board, especially Bradley's fellow Republicans.

The cabin belonged to a friend of Bradley's; he didn't say who, and she didn't press for more. Before they left, they ran the sheets through the wash and hung them on a line outside. Over the summer they worked on the breakfast plan. Between the two of them they met with every board member individually, pitching the breakfast program in language designed to make that particular board member like the idea. They identified cuts that would make Republicans happy and that Democrats could convince themselves to live with. They lined up support from Pastor Fred, from the chamber of commerce, from the *Herald*. All this time, they didn't sleep together. Maybe, she thought, it was over.

In August she and Art drove their car behind Michael's car to Asheville, got him settled in his dorm room, and hugged him goodbye. Afterward, they wandered the campus together in silence, wondering how time had passed so quickly. Back at home she missed his foods in the fridge, his shoes cluttering the foyer, the layered clouds of teenage stink that wafted from his room after stretches of particularly intense neglect. He called every few days, sounding flat and lost, and they knew he was struggling. For them, college had been a joyous liberation from unhappy families to which they never returned, but Michael's childhood had been happy—hadn't it? Maybe, for him, liberation wasn't as tantalizing. She'd always been proud of her relationship with her son—always felt that she knew him better than the average mother of a teenage boy. But now she wondered if that might have been an illusion. He'd been gone for only a month, but it felt like much longer. A whole era. Every day she wanted him back, and every day she wanted him to be okay where he was, and every day she wondered if this was how she would feel forever.

* * *

As soon as she heard him drive off, she called. They could talk. It could be contained. How? Somehow. No answer. Bradley left but came right back, red faced and shouting about his truck. He didn't even knock. She almost had to push him out the door, insisting they would talk later, that he had to leave. Now. She tried calling again. No answer. She threw herself into erasing every physical trace, real or imagined, of Bradley's presence in the house. Stripped the bed. Put the sheets and pillowcases in the wash. Did the dishes. Vacuumed the carpet at the top of the stairs, then the carpet in the bedroom, and then the rest of the house, always making sure the home phone and her cell phone were both nearby. She took a shower, scrubbing off every particle of Bradley and what they'd done together, sliding open the shower door every half minute or so to check the two phones, which she'd put on a towel on the floor, both set to ring at the highest possible volume. After the shower she changed into pajamas, moved the sheets and pillowcases to the dryer, put her towel and Art's towel and her purple robe in the wash. She went into Michael's room, as if she might find something there that could calm her down, and she was sitting on his bed when she called him the third time, and again got no answer, and again hung up before the end of his voicemail message. On Sunday night Art came back, unpacked his suitcase, and went to sleep early. Just before he fell asleep, he thanked her for cleaning the house.

On Tuesday she leaves work early, stops by Genova's, orders an egg salad sandwich to go, makes some small talk with Sam, and drives home, where right away she takes out a yellow legal pad and three pens: one black, one blue, one red. She makes a cup of tea, sits at the kitchen table, and forces her eyes shut, attempting to quiet everything but the task in front of her. Quiet the unfolded laundry. Quiet the imminent need to replace the water heater, to read the *Consumer Reports* article about how to pick a water heater. Quiet the fact that she has called Michael six times in four days. The fact that he hasn't answered. The look she keeps convincing herself she sees on Art's face. Quiet everything but one question: how to most effectively use her time at tomorrow night's public school board meeting to sell the new budget to the citizens of Yew County—or, in truth, to the small percentage of them who bother following school board business.

This is not just selfishness, she tells herself. She is not just looking for a break from the torture of reviewing her own mistakes. The work she wants to do—the work she will start doing if she can make her mind quiet enough—is important. Objectively important. A better school budget will make Yew County a better place. Make people's lives unambiguously better. Children's lives. Parents' lives. Surely this justifies turning away from the mess of her life for a few hours.

On the blank top page of the legal pad, she writes, with the blue pen: *This is not meant to be the final word on next year's budget. It's meant to be a starting point. That's why we're releasing it almost six months before it's due. Now we need your feedback.*

She underlines *your* with the red pen. *Your feedback.* She tears off the piece of paper. She crumples it. On the next piece, she writes a list of everything the draft budget accomplishes, then tears that piece off, too, but doesn't crumple it. On the next piece of paper, using the blue pen, she writes words that she thinks might help frame those accomplishments in a way that appeals to an archetypal Yew County Republican with an interest in school board business. She tears this piece off, too, and on the next piece does the same exercise, but for Democrats. Then she tears that list off and sets the three lists—accomplishments, Republican framing words, Democratic framing words—side by side and lets her eyes roam between them. She nibbles on her egg salad sandwich, idly wondering how many Genova's egg salad sandwiches she's eaten over the years.

She tries to let the right words come.

Tries to push away the memory of Michael standing just a few feet from where she's sitting. The disgust on his face.

Is this made more difficult by the fact that the budget is just as much Bradley's project as hers? That it's *their* project?

Of course.

But there's nothing to do about that now. She's a fool, and she's made a mess—but these aren't reasons to abandon a good budget.

It isn't the perfect budget. It isn't everything that she would ask for, were she able to snap her fingers and get whatever she wanted. But it is better—much better, she is absolutely sure—than anything else that could possibly pass, and much better than anything that would be on the table had she and Bradley not put it there.

She clicks to retract the tip of the blue pen. Clicks to extend it again. On the new top sheet of the legal pad, she writes:

This budget commits us to making sure all of Springwater's children start the day on a full stomach. Crosses it out. *This plan makes us a district where no child starts the day distracted by hunger.* Crosses it out. *When all children in our district have breakfasts, they all have the chance to succeed.* Crosses it out. It feels good to work: to let everything slip away, to move toward the moment when all that remains is exactly what she wants to say, exactly how she wants to say it.

When every child in our district has breakfast, we all get better value and less waste from our tax dollars.

When all the children in our district get to eat—

Her cell phone buzzes on the table and she peers over to read the caller ID: LINDA/ROBERT HOME. She decides to let it go to voicemail.

When every child in our district starts the day with breakfast, it actually benefits—

Now the landline rings. She considers ignoring it in the name of maintaining her concentration. The only reason she gets up is because of the chance, however small, that it's Michael, finally calling her back.

LINDA/ROBERT HOME.

Inertia takes over. "Hello?"

It's Robert; right away he asks if Art is home. And then Linda is on the line too—on another handset, it sounds like—also asking if Art is home. "Have you heard of a company called Arcadian Airlines?" says Linda. "It's not really a company. It's a shell company, and it's—but, well, have you heard of it?"

"I don't think so."

"Are you sure?"

"Pretty sure."

"Well. It's in Springwater."

— **85** —

"Okay."

"Your Springwater."

"Okay."

"It's the CIA," says Linda. "It's the CIA flying these flights. Torture flights. There's going to be a story in the *Times*. Can you believe it? Springwater in the *New York Times*? Can we come for dinner tomorrow? Or Thursday? There's a lot to talk about."

After they've hung up, she sits back at the kitchen table and stares at the torn-out legal pad sheets—accomplishments, Republican framing words, Democratic framing words— hoping to pick up where she left off. But she's shut out now. She stands up and walks back to the living room. She's still holding the phone. She walks to the little alcove in the back of the house that they have always called "the office," giving it three or four more notches of dignity than it deserves. She sits at the computer and googles. *CIA Arcadian Airlines, Springwater torture, CIA Springwater shell company, Springwater torture flights,* variation after variation—nothing. She googles *Yew County Airport* and it looks like she remembers it: a single-story brick building, a few aluminum hangars, and just one runway. She googles *torture flights* and the photographs come up. The naked men, the pyramid, the hood. She's seen them before, whenever they were in the news. She doesn't look closely and doesn't click to make them bigger. She closes the web browser.

Tuesdays are the only day of the week when Art still does one-on-one counseling, which means that on a usual Tuesday night they don't say much to each other; after six hours of talk therapy, he's done talking. It takes time for the day's conversations to loosen their hold on him, for anything new to be allowed in. She says nothing about Linda and Robert's call when he first gets home, nothing about it when he opens his beer, nothing about it for their first several minutes at the dinner table together. She waits as long as she can. "Robert and Linda called today," she says.

He looks up from his plate. "Oh?"

She tries her best to relay what they said. She doesn't know if *torture* is a word she's ever said, out loud, to him or anyone else. She remembers hearing, back in Durham, about torture—but as far as she can remember, that torture was in South America.

"How do they even know about this?" says Art.

"They didn't say."

"How do they know what's going to be in the *Times*?"

"I don't know."

"Arcadian." Art says it again, slower—*Ar-ca-di-an*—like a new word from a foreign language. "Never heard of it."

"Me neither."

"And what do you think they mean, *a lot to talk about*?"

"I don't know."

He takes a sip of beer and says something soft that she hears as "Heard from Michael today."

Everything inside her freezes. "What?"

"I said, did you hear from Michael today?"

"Oh. No. Why?"

"Just wondering. It seems like he's already calling less and less."

"Well, I don't know," she says. "Maybe he's making friends."

"Or falling in love."

"Maybe. Maybe he's being seduced by a charming grad student."

"Is that what happened?"

"As I recall, yes."

"Well, if so—lucky her."

"So, can they come for dinner on Thursday?"

"Sure, sure."

Once the dishwasher is running, she packs herself tomorrow's lunch, which is really just snacks she'll be able to eat in her car if she has to. Carrots, hummus, nuts, a hard-boiled egg. She can hear that Art is in the office, and has the urge to go ask what he's doing. But she leaves him alone. It's Tuesday.

Later, though, when he's upstairs getting ready for bed, she goes to the office and turns the computer back on and checks the browser history. She's never checked the browser history before, and only knows it's an option thanks to an article she read over the summer in her dentist's waiting room: "How to Find Out If Your Teen Is Using Online Pornography." Michael was still home then, but she had no temptation to snoop on his browser history. She remembers feeling superior to other mothers—superior to their panics about what their sons were up to, the kind of men the world was turning them into.

She clicks to open the web browser. Because she can't explain what she's doing, she doesn't exactly believe that she's doing it. She's watching herself in a movie, waiting to see what the character named Mel decides. She pulls up the browser history. *Arcadian Airlines, CIA Springwater, torture flights.*

Upstairs she finds Art already asleep, a sci-fi paperback splayed open on his chest, rising and falling with his breath. She's grateful. She doesn't have to figure out what to say or not say, doesn't have to wonder what he is sensing or not sensing in her facial expression, in her posture, in the air between them. Because he's asleep, it's possible to feel that nothing is going unsaid. She's just standing in her bedroom, watching her husband rest.

* * *

The next evening she arrives at the high school ten minutes early.

All day she has resisted calling Michael again—and now, sitting in her car, she gives in. "Michael, it's your mom. Call me back, please. Even if you're busy, just call back to let me know you're all right."

Being at the high school feels different, knowing he's hundreds of miles away.

Inside she goes to the auditorium and heads straight to the stage, where, as always, three long folding tables have been set end to end so all nine board members can face the audience. She takes her usual spot: third from the right on what is, by unspoken rule, the Democrats' side. She sees Sheila's purse in Sheila's usual chair, fourth from the right. She spots Bradley in the audience, talking with a couple she doesn't recognize, laughing warmly at something the husband just said.

She spots Pastor Fred, sitting by himself at the far end of a row of chairs toward the front of the auditorium. Their eyes meet, and he gives her a quick little nod.

The meeting starts. She's grateful that Bradley's seat is four down from hers, and even more grateful that it is perfectly within the bounds of normal behavior for the two of them to more or less ignore each other.

Mel gives her introduction and decides on the spot to use the line about how *subsidized breakfasts unlock value from tax dollars.* All the other board members say a few words, everyone commending everyone else for their willingness to compromise. Some draw attention to a favorite feature or two of the draft, but everyone avoids hammering too hard on anything specific. Thanks to Bradley's nudges, all the Republicans think that they're the side getting more of what they want. Thanks to Mel's nudges, all the Democrats think the opposite. Each side is aware of what the other thinks, but each side thinks the other is wrong. Both sides are happy.

There's something dreamlike about the fact that it's actually happening. That they're actually one step closer to putting breakfast in the stomachs of students who would otherwise go without breakfast.

What looks to Mel like thirty members of the public have shown up, and somehow none of them voice any serious objections. Of course, objections could come later. But it's undeniable: things are going well. Pastor Fred keeps shooting her a look—and he's probably shooting the same look to Bradley—that means he's not sure what to do. He'd agreed to come and offer remarks to calm people's objections, using the authority of his position to make feeding children sound simultaneously like the Christian thing to do, the conservative thing to do, and the liberal thing to do. But now no objections are materializing. He gets up and says a few words anyway, which is a good thing, because a *Herald* reporter has shown up, and a quote from Pastor Fred stands a good chance of making the story.

In slightly different circumstances, she and Bradley would surely find a way to share a quick second of celebratory eye contact. But tonight she looks either out toward the back of the auditorium or down at her legal pad. It feels impossible to calibrate a shared glance that unambiguously celebrates just the budget (and all their tiny budget-related deceptions) and not the sex (and all their tiny sex-related deceptions).

Afterward, in the lobby, she tries to duck out and get to the parking lot as quickly as possible. No chitchat tonight. But Pastor Fred cuts her off. "Sorry," he says. "I wasn't sure what to do back there. I hope that was okay. Was that okay?"

"Of course, it was great."

"You're sure?"

"More than sure."

"Great. I just got nervous, you know?"

"Completely natural," she says. "You did great."

Art is sitting in the living room. On the coffee table in front of him: a Miller Lite and several stacks of paper.

"Meeting good?"

"Meeting good."

"Big win for you and the khaki collaborator?"

"Big win."

"Well, good." He likes teasing her about Bradley, though for whatever reason he always calls him Brad. *Your khaki collaborator. Your Republican partner in crime.* Sometimes, when he knows they're meeting alone together, he makes her promise not to come back transformed into a Springwater Country Club wife or reciting the virtues of lower marginal tax rates. But he's only joking. Whenever she presses him, he reassures her: because she's willing to work with Brad, good things are happening in the district that wouldn't happen otherwise. Life is complicated. Getting things done is hard.

She points at the stacks of paper. "What's this?"

"Oh, you know. Torture flights."

She takes off her shoes and joins him on the couch. "Did you call Robert today?"

"No. I probably should have. I guess I wanted to do some

of my own reading first, you know? Is that dumb? You know how they are."

"I know how Linda is."

"Exactly, yeah."

"Any word from Michael?"

"Nope."

They sit together and take turns with the printouts, reading about men kept in cells, kept awake without light, with constant light, with noise. Moved from cell to cell. Kept without clothes, without soap, without water, beaten, slapped, water poured into their lungs, locked in closets too short to stand up in, locked in coffins. Told they were about to be executed, pistols cocked behind their head, pressed up against their skulls. Hanged from the ceilings. Told their wives and children were about to be executed. Had already been executed. Been raped. Left alone for hours, days. The only sounds are Art tapping his pen against his paper, and the occasional press of the pen against the paper as he circles something or makes a check mark. At some point she gets up and makes tea.

When was the last time they read together like this?

She curls into her husband and attempts to beam a silent promise to the universe: if only everything can work out—if only she can be allowed to fix this—she will never try to get away with anything ever again. If only it can all be made to go away, she will for the rest of her life do nothing but honor and appreciate what she already has.

Before bed she emails Pastor Fred, apologizing for rushing through their conversation in the lobby and thanking him again for his support. Then she sees a new message has arrived, from a person whose name she doesn't recognize, Eunice Larabee:

Melanie Kinston,

I had been hoping to speak to you at tonight's school board meeting, but you left so quickly afterward. I wonder if it was because you are embarrassed by the budget you are apparently backing, you should be. I voted for you, because I wanted a real Democrat on the board to fight off these vultures who do not even believe in public ed and only join the board to keep the school down. (Also I wanted to vote for a woman too if she was qualified.) But now you are backing this crazy plan that will take soooo much money out of the classroom and lead to more teachers leaving the state, I don't get it. Can't you see that when you are on the same side as a country club oldboy like Bradley Welk it is time to take a good look in the mirror? And then you don't even stick around to listen to what real people have to say about it. I'm sorry but that just doesn't sit with me. You can talk about compromise but you can only compromise so much. I was going to wait to write until tomorrow but I cannot sleep I am so upset so I am writing to you now. I hope you will reconsider your vote and do better going forward when it comes to listening to the real people who put you in office.

Sincerely,
Eunice Larabee

While she is reading Eunice's email, another one arrives, this one from her son: *Stop calling me.*

* * *

For dinner with Robert and Linda, she makes pork chops and roasted potatoes. Of her five most reliable meals, this is the easiest to prepare. But it's also Michael's favorite, and as the smell of the cooking fills the kitchen and then the entire first floor, she regrets her choice.

"What is it?" says Art. "What's wrong?"

"I made pork chops." She doesn't need to say anything else; he understands. They hold each other in the middle of the kitchen, surrounded by the heat from the oven and the smell of their son's favorite meal.

"Did he call today?" he says.

"No."

She is sure that Art doesn't know—that he couldn't possibly know and still hold her so gently.

How strange to see Linda and Robert's car pull into their driveway and know that tonight, for the first time in years, they will be talking politics again.

In the foyer, Robert makes a show of cocking his head and sniffing like a curious dog. "Your chops?"

"My chops."

He puts his hands together and tilts his head up toward the ceiling in prayerful thanks. "I didn't dare hope."

Mel assumes that Linda will, as soon as possible, launch right into things, peppering them with facts and *did-you-knows* and *isn't-it-horribles*. But she's wrong. Instead, once they sit down, Linda and Robert ask how Michael's doing at school, how they're doing with their empty nest. They seem genuinely curious, but Mel can't help wondering if this was a plan they formulated ahead of time. (The scene isn't hard to imagine: Robert counseling Linda to *go easy*, to *not come on too strong*, to *remember they're not like they used to be.*) They talk about the heaviness of the drive back from Asheville. "You see it in movies and it's a cliché," says Art. "But then it's your turn."

"He's settling in?" says Robert.

"We haven't heard from him for a few days," says Art. "But that must be normal. That's normal, right?"

"Of course," says Linda. "Of course it is."

"We're trying not to read into it," says Mel.

"Good luck," says Robert.

It ends up being Art who moves the conversation down its preordained track. "So, tell us about Arcadian Airlines."

Robert does most of the explaining. He's probably a good professor: the information comes efficiently and clearly, and she never feels herself in danger of losing the plot. She wonders if he and Linda agreed beforehand that he would be the one to explain. If he made her promise not to interrupt.

Springwater is the hiding place for a CIA shell corporation that transports people to torture dungeons around the world.

It pretends to be just another charter flight company.

But it's not.

"You can call them up and ask for a flight," Robert says, "and they just say they're all booked."

What he's saying feels so strange that, coming from someone else, it might be easy to reject or doubt. But because it's Robert, they don't.

They learned about it from a friend, Robert says, a lawyer who does pro bono work for detainees.

"Locals sign the incorporation papers," says Linda. "But it's a scam. They're just shielding the CIA."

"What's in it for them?" says Art.

"Who knows?" says Robert. "Some probably think it's the patriotic thing. Or they like the excitement, maybe. I don't know. Maybe they get paid."

"And you've definitely never heard of Arcadian Airlines?" says Linda.

"No," says Art. "Never." He asks whether this means that any torturers are themselves living here in Springwater. This possibility had not occurred to Mel, and it moves through her like fine cracks branching out through a sheet of lake-top ice.

Robert says that they don't know for sure but they don't think so. The evidence they have shows the flights that leave Springwater almost always make pickup stops in D.C. before heading overseas, indicating that the people living in Spring-water are only pilots. "But we really don't know," he says. "Maybe Keith will figure it out."

Keith, explains Linda, is the *Times* reporter working on a piece that will inform the public of everything they've been talking about. "He's such a nice guy. He says it should run sometime in the next month."

"We're hoping," says Robert, "that when the story comes out people are going to be pretty angry. And we're hoping—"

"We're hoping to plan an action," says Linda. "Here, in Springwater. With your help."

"You don't have to say anything now," says Robert. "Of course, you'll want to think about it, talk about it. But—"

"Definitely," says Linda. "Don't decide now. But we wanted to tell you."

Mel can't believe she didn't see it coming. Once upon a

time, she would have known from the start. When something was wrong, you joined an action. If there wasn't an action to join, you made your own.

"What kind of action?" says Art.

"We don't know," says Robert. "That's what we want your help with."

"Like old times," says Linda.

Mel is surprised to feel a lump in her throat. She can see it's the same for the others: the lump, the surprising presence of their younger selves.

Dessert: ice cream sandwiches and decaf in the living room. An ease between the four of them that Mel hasn't felt for years. Again she prays: *Let my mistakes go unpunished, and I will not make them again.*

"There's one more thing," says Linda. "Something you should know."

Robert has his coffee mug halfway to his mouth, and he stops it there, switches course, sets it back on the table. "Well, we're not—"

"It's supposed to be a secret. But just for now. We're going to tell you, but we're not supposed to tell you yet."

"Not because we don't trust you," says Robert. "Just because . . . it's complicated."

"But," says Linda, "I feel like we should be able to trust our oldest friends."

Mel can tell from the look on Robert's face that he doesn't think it's a good idea, but also that he knows it's going to happen anyway. "You don't need to tell us," she says, though she can feel herself already anticipating the burst of shared warmth that will come from the secret—whatever it is— being pierced, its boundaries being reconfigured in real time around them.

"Oh, we'll definitely tell you," Robert says. "We want to tell you. We're just not supposed—"

"I think we can tell them," says Linda. "I think we should."

"Well," says Robert. "If you think so."

"Whatever feels right," says Art. "Don't stress about it."

"As long as you can promise to not tell anyone," says Linda. "Do you promise?"

"Promise," she and Art say in unintentional unison.

"I mean it. Not anybody."

"We promise, we promise," says Art. "What is it?"

"Well," says Robert. "It's about this one particular person. Someone you know. Bradley Welk."

"Holy shit, Brad?" says Art. "Is Brad one of the owners? Or the pretend owners, or whatever they are?"

Robert nods, grimacing. "On paper, he's the president. Now, Mel, we know you're on the school board together."

She tells herself she's allowed to be shocked—that what she's hearing would count as shocking even if her interactions with Bradley were limited to school board business. The question is how shocked, exactly. How shocked would an innocent person look? "How do you know?"

"We googled," says Linda.

"No, I mean—how do you know he's with Arcadian?"

"His name's right there on the papers," says Robert.

"Jesus," says Art. "Brad. Fuck."

"Melly?" says Linda. "Are you okay?"

She has to say something. "Yeah. It's just—like Art said, it's a shock. I mean, we've been working all summer on this new budget plan."

"Isn't he a Republican?" says Linda. "We read online that—"

"That's how things actually get passed here, you work with Republicans."

"Of course," says Linda, leaning over and putting a hand on her knee. "Of course. But you can keep it secret, right? Like you promised?"

"Of course," she says. "Of course I can."

"I knew you worked together, but I didn't know you . . . *worked* together."

By the time they leave, she's sure Art knows. She's terrified to be alone with him—to hear what he'll say, what he will reveal himself to already know, or suspect, what question he will launch at her, and how she will answer.

"How you doing?" he says.

"Just . . . shocked."

"It's shocking."

"It's going to be hard," she says. "To see him. It's going to be . . . hard."

"We'll figure it out."

"We'll figure it out?"

"We'll figure it out."

Floss, brush teeth, gargle mouthwash. Give the sink a quick wipe.

In one of Art's printouts, she read about men in one of the prisons, she can't remember which prison, being forced to strip naked and masturbate together while their guards filmed.

One afternoon in the spring she drove an hour to Raleigh and found her way to a hotel whose name Bradley had sent her the night before in a text message. Right after letting her into the room, he pulled her clothes off while she was still standing, then pushed her down on the bed and told her to touch herself while he watched. No one had ever asked or told her to do that before, she had never thought about being asked or told to do that, let alone imagined how wildly alive it would make her feel to be doing it, how intensely deep inside of herself and at the same time outside of herself it would feel, the pleasure of the juxtaposition.

When exactly was it, that afternoon at the hotel? When was it in relationship to whenever the photographs—the naked men, the pyramids, the hoods—started coming out? Was it possible that because of his connection to this company, Arcadian Airlines, Bradley had somehow seen the photos *before* then? It was not the last time he told her to touch herself, and not the last time she did as he said.

The mental act of trying to push it all away only brings it closer, which makes her push harder, which pulls it closer.

What if Art wants sex tonight? She can only imagine it as a nightmare. Sex with her husband bleeding together with sex with Bradley bleeding together with the photographs. But if he comes asking, she doesn't want to turn him down. Not tonight.

Thankfully, he's already asleep. Instantly her desire to be excused from the question of whether to have sex with him is replaced by the desire for him to wake up and demand to know exactly what she is thinking, to say that he knows she's keeping a secret, to insist on his right to know, to keep insisting until she tells him everything. But no. He stays sleeping. He's always been a heavy sleeper. She would have to literally yell his name to wake him up, which she doesn't think she's going to do. And she's right: she doesn't.

AMIRA

They met at the pizza counter behind the Vittorio Emanuele metro stop: she was in line, he was working the oven, smiling like nothing in the world could make him happier. She thought she felt something—a mutual curiosity hanging in the air, waiting to be put to use. "What's your favorite?" she called out.

"Me?" He turned to face her. For the first time since she'd come through the door, he was still—not sliding something in or out of the oven, not consolidating pizza from two trays onto one, not adjusting the tiny signs identifying toppings and flavors. He recommended the artichoke—not the artichoke with tomato sauce, the artichoke with just cheese—and also the sausage.

"So," said the listless cashier. "One of each?"

There was no indoor seating. She wished she'd noticed which pizzas were fresh from the oven and which weren't, and that she'd ordered from those that weren't, so she could have stood there longer while they reheated, creating more time for something to happen.

Too late.

She sat at a scuffed white plastic table, ate her pizza, and wondered if he might come outside to talk to her, and if maybe she'd been imagining things, and how long she was prepared to wait. Just when she was about to leave, the door opened and he came through.

He nodded at her empty plate. "Well?"

She told him she'd enjoyed the artichoke but found the sausage a little too sweet.

"Serves me right," he said. He'd never actually had the sausage, and recommended it only because it was the store's top seller. "I shouldn't have sold you something I'd never tried myself. I apologize."

"It's fine," she said. "After all, I ate it. And like you said, it's the top seller. How could you have known?"

He pointed out that he could have said: *The sausage is our top seller, but I've never actually had it.* That would have been honest. Or he could have told her his real second favorite: the olive and ricotta. He offered to go back inside and get her a piece, no charge. She told him not to. She was full. And anyway, she didn't want him to leave.

One afternoon months later, as they lay naked together in bed, he told her that on the day they'd met, he wasn't supposed to have been at the counter. He'd already started working at the butcher stall, where he got more hours and better pay. But early that morning—before dawn, even—he got a phone call from his former coworker Arsalan, complaining that he'd been up all night with stomach problems, maybe food poisoning, and didn't think he'd be able to make it in to start the oven that morning. Could Ayoub cover?

If this had happened just a month earlier, Ayoub explained, he likely would have said no. Or said yes but been miserable about it. For years he'd felt he never got enough sleep, and never made enough money, and that these two facts were intimately connected. He moved from one shared apartment to another, places where he slept and ate and washed himself but never truly relaxed. He was always fighting just to stay afloat, always worried that if he stopped fighting for even a second, he would sink and drown. Under these conditions, being woken in the middle of a night meant more than just insufficient sleep. It meant being reminded of the bigger problem: insufficient everything.

But on this particular morning, talking to Arsalan on the phone, he found himself happier than he'd been in years. Things were good at the butcher's. He'd been there only long enough to get paid once, but that already meant more money in his pocket than he was used to. He liked being away from the heat of the pizza oven. He was sleeping better; he felt rested and able to help a man in need, a fellow immigrant. Perhaps, he thought, the era of insufficient everything was ending. Perhaps a new era was beginning. An era of more.

Walking his old route to work, starting the oven, getting the pizzas going, setting up for the day to come: just a week earlier, he'd been spending his shifts silently celebrating that soon he would never have to do any of these things ever again. Now, though, the familiar tasks and rhythms of the place brought him pleasure, and noticing this aspect of his experience intensified it; seeing himself pleased made him more pleased. Of all the days he ever spent at the counter, this was probably the best—even before the beautiful Italian woman walked in. He watched through the window while she ate out front. He prayed that, for whatever reason, she would still be there at the end of his shift. He promised himself that if she was still there when he was done, he would do something.

Everything that came after would have been delightful no

matter when it had happened. But looking back, he saw it had been extra delightful thanks to the emotional momentum of his day. This didn't occur to him at the time; in the moment, his happiness was so complete, and so shocking, that all he could do was make sure he gave it his full attention. Only later, as the days had passed and he'd thought obsessively about their meeting, had he come up with this fuller theory.

"Is this too much?" he said, pulling back so they could see each other's faces.

All her apartment mates were out for the afternoon. Sunlight and sunbaked air were floating through the bedroom's open window. "Is what too much?" she said.

"Saying all this. I don't know."

"I love it."

And she did. Lying there naked, listening to him dissect what he'd felt and why: it was pure pleasure. She'd never known a man who talked like that. She loved hearing it, loved taking what he said and applying it retrospectively to her own memory of their meeting, adding new colors and depth, turning it this way and that to see how it looked from different angles.

She'd been in Esquilino that day because she'd been getting bored. After eleven years in the city, it no longer excited her like it once had. For the first few years she'd been carried along by the energy of arrival. Then: a few years of enjoying her fluency with the place. Lately, though, she'd found herself missing a certain sense of possibility: the ambient knowledge that an adventure of one kind or another—even just a quiet, private one—might at any moment spark itself into existence. The point wasn't really how often such adventures actually happened. The point was feeling, on a given day, that they *could* happen. She knew memory was tricky, but still: she was sure she used to have this feeling more. She missed it. And so she'd gone out wandering, trying to find it.

She'd said little about this to Ayoub, not because she thought it was at all shameful or embarrassing, but because of the possibility, skittering around the back of her head, that to say something would create the impression that her interest was less in Ayoub the real person and more in Ayoub the symbol of difference. A new thing. A discovery. Foreign. She'd tried to ask herself as directly as she could whether this was possibly the case, and felt strongly that the answer was almost certainly no, and definitely more no than yes. But she didn't want to risk planting the possibility in his mind. She'd also said nothing to him about the pleasure that she took from his Italian, which was impressively fluent—he'd taken classes for years—and also woven through with a thousand little differences that conspired to give his sentences a captivating singsong musicality. Instead of saying anything about how much she enjoyed it, she just enjoyed it and kept the enjoyment to herself.

The day after their wedding, they moved into an apartment they'd found that made both their trips to work shorter. "So we can spend more time in bed," he said. "Even on workdays." Neither of them had been opposed to living together sooner, but it hadn't been easy to find a place they liked, could afford, and could imagine staying with a child. Their life together was, she thought, the best thing she'd ever made herself a part of. Looking back on her previous romantic relationships—even the best of them, the longest lasting and most passionate—she saw a woman (herself, or the self that had once been her) and a man throwing themselves against each other to see what happened, how good it was or wasn't, and whether it was worth repeating the process. With Ayoub it was different: they were making something together, something new, and doing it together was changing them.

Like all couples, they made private codes and rituals: afternoon cappuccinos, tonnarelli alla Ayoub, various lovemaking routines. He bought her little presents. Not the clichés—not jewelry and flowers, or not *just* jewelry and flowers, the way it was with some men, where bracelets and roses were evidence less of affection than of a poor imagination, or a desire to show off what they could afford. He bought her refrigerator magnets he knew she would find cute or funny; her favorite was a fat furry dog with horn-rimmed spectacles. He got her little notebooks. And DVDs: Moroccan movies, Egyptian movies, Italian movies, American movies. He got her a vegetable peeler with two ends: one produced normal peelings, the other made thin strips. For some reason they named the peeler, and for some reason they picked the name Eduardo.

All her friends from before—classmates, apartment mates, neighbors—dropped her. It hurt, but she wondered why it didn't hurt more. Maybe, she thought, life with Ayoub was so good that it was easy for her heart to understand that anyone who didn't approve simply didn't understand anything, didn't understand life, and so wasn't worth wanting—or missing—as a friend. Meeting Meryem probably helped. But she couldn't avoid thinking that she would have been fine anyway: that the core energy of her life was so good, and so powerful, that it could carry her through anything.

* * *

Three days before their one-year wedding anniversary, Ayoub came home from work and told her that he'd run into Arsalan and invited him to dinner.

"Tonight?"

"Tonight, yeah."

"You didn't want to check with me first?"

"It's just dinner."

She'd tried going back, looking for the moment—the hour, the day, the week—when things had changed between them. But she'd never been able to find it, and she suspected that the work of putting their every interaction under the microscope, magnifying every potential flaw, had made things feel even worse.

"Is he one of your 'flat men'?"

"Don't call them that," he said.

"I'm not the one who calls them that. You are. That's why I put it in quotes."

"But you didn't put it in quotes."

"I did, with my voice."

"I'll call and cancel," said Ayoub. "I'll tell him to forget it."

"No. It's fine." Maybe, she thought, a dinner like this was just what they needed. From the beginning of their marriage, Ayoub had enjoyed having his old coworkers and apartment mates over for dinner, especially the "flat men" among them. She liked it, too; it was the type of thing Ayoub wished more people had done for him during his hard years, so she sometimes felt like she was reaching back in time to help that younger Ayoub. She liked watching the men soften a little— unflatten—in the warmth of their company. It made them feel like a family and made their house feel like a home.

Perhaps by showing Arsalan what a happy couple they could be, they might be reminded of this fact themselves. Ayoub hadn't talked to Arsalan for over a year, since the day he'd covered for him at the pizza counter—the day she'd wandered in. Even if someone had told Arsalan about his old coworker's marriage, he likely had no idea about his small but pivotal role. They would tell him. He would be pleased; who wouldn't be pleased to learn something like that? And when he left, they would feel better.

At first, Arsalan seemed to her the exact definition of a flat man: quiet and withdrawn, unsure of how to conduct himself at a family dinner table. She reminded herself to be sympathetic. Who knew what a decade could do to a man? Who knew how Ayoub himself would have ended up in a just slightly different world?

But soon she detected something else, a more intentional iciness.

She tried telling the story of her and Ayoub's meeting, but from the start Arsalan responded not with the participatory delight that she'd anticipated but instead with the air of a man who has gone out to a park bench for his lunch hour and, finding himself pestered by an unsavory stranger, attempts to make the best of things by pretending the stranger isn't there. She kept signaling to Ayoub that he should take over, but he either didn't understand the signals or refused to help. By the time she was done, she couldn't avoid the thought that she might never want to tell the story again.

Later, after they'd eaten, Arsalan asked her his first direct question. "What's your real name, signora?" It came out with the pressurized intensity of something he'd done his best to hold in but was now forced to release, a failure for which he seemed to blame her more than himself.

"You mean the name I used before Amira?" She'd decided long ago that the name question wasn't inherently rude, but she wished more people would use their imagination enough to realize that, while it might be harmless in itself, it was unpleasant to be asked again and again—especially in a tone like the one Arsalan was using, a tone that suggested he thought he was about to catch her in some lie.

"Yes, that's what I mean. Your name from your parents."

"Maria," she said.

"You were Catholic?"

"I suppose so. By default."

"But not now. Now you're Muslim."

"Well, yes, in some sense." She looked at Ayoub: *Intervene.*

"In some sense?" said Arsalan.

"Yes. Just as my husband is." She gave Ayoub another look: *I know you know I just asked you to intervene, and I won't let you deny it later.* "I'm just as much a Muslim as I ever was a Catholic, anyway."

"What does being Muslim mean to you?"

"What does it mean to you, Arsalan?" she said. She gave Ayoub one last look: *Damn you.* "Do you have a checklist of what it means to be a 'real Muslim'? Have you come for dinner or to interrogate me? And what about my husband—why aren't you asking him these questions? Why only me?"

"I didn't mean—"

"So you say. But—"

"I was only curious, signora."

"If you say so." She stood up and started gathering dishes. "I'll bring tea out in a bit."

From the kitchen, she could hear that they were talking

but couldn't make out what they were saying. She wanted not to care, but she couldn't help it. "For me," she whispered to herself, "being a Muslim means taking part in some of the beautiful and moving traditions my husband grew up with, and using them as a way to be with God's plans and mysteries." She thought she was starting to make out a pattern in the sounds from the next room: Ayoub asking questions, Arsalan answering. Were they talking softly to avoid her hearing? Maybe Arsalan had started it—the soft talking—and Ayoub had followed his lead. He could be considerate like that, when he wasn't being horrible. Remembering this fact cooled her rage and, simultaneously, stoked it. He had the power to be considerate. And he was choosing not to use it. He'd abandoned her.

Eventually, her curiosity became stronger than her resentment. She made a tray of tea and cookies, took it out to the table, and sat down again. "What are we talking about?"

Her husband smiled—but the smile was tight and false. "Arsalan was just telling me about Pakistan. About some business he does there."

"What kind of business?"

"Oh," said Arsalan. "Just . . . business." He looked at his watch. "I should go, though. After all, I'm opening the pizza counter tomorrow."

At the door, he thanked them both for having him: for the first time that evening, Amira felt he was saying something to her that he actually meant.

"Being a Muslim, for me," she heard herself saying, "means I take part in traditions my husband grew up with, which I find beautiful and moving, and which strengthen my faith in God."

He looked confused, like he'd forgotten about badgering

her earlier. "Good," he said. "That's . . . good." He turned to Ayoub. "Think about what I said. For your family. And for yourself, too."

She assumed that once Arsalan was gone, Ayoub would right away start explaining what they'd been talking about. When no explanation came, she refused to ask for one. She cleaned the dishes, swept the kitchen floor, turned out the lights—and no explanation came.

"Was he always like that?" she asked when they were in bed together.

"Like what?"

"Like, so rude?"

"I told you," he said. "These men don't get to socialize much. They eat alone. They get used to it. We shouldn't judge."

"I'm not judging. I'm asking. Was he like that when you worked together?"

"It's hard to say at work, Amira."

"Why are you mad at me?"

"I'm not mad at you."

"What was it he wanted you to think about? He wants our money? For his 'business'?"

"It's complicated."

"Go ahead."

It wasn't, in the end, very complicated at all. Arsalan lived cheaply, saving almost all the money he made at the pizza counter so that, once or twice a year, he could travel to Pakistan, see family, and visit the jewelry markets in Lahore, where he bought as much as he could fit in the two suitcases he was allowed on his return flight. Over time, he'd come to know jewelry buyers and sellers all across Rome, from high-end stores to smaller stalls. He'd recently started commissioning Italian-style jewelry for them, increasing his profits—which, on each subsequent visit to Lahore, he used to buy more silver.

"And what, he wants you to invest? Is it even legal?"

"Why wouldn't it be?"

"What about customs?"

"I'm sure he knows the rules."

"Okay, well."

"And that's just half of it." Over the last two years, Ayoub explained, Arsalan had made these trips to Pakistan longer, adding extra days so that he could drive north to see two of his cousins. These cousins worked as administrators of camps built for Afghan refugees. Ever since the attacks on America, international aid had been declining, even though, thanks to the American bombs dropping on Afghanistan, the camps were operating at full capacity. From each jewelry sale, Arsalan set aside money, which he delivered to his cousins and helped them put to use: tracking down a new water pump, for example, or driving somewhere to pick up a discounted shipment of sanitary supplies. There was always something to do.

"So it's two in one," Ayoub said. "He's making money, and doing charity for Muslims in need."

She saw on his face that he thought he'd surprised her: that this was a turn she hadn't expected, and that the new information ran counter to the picture of Arsalan she'd been developing in her mind. And yes, she *was* surprised. But did he have to gloat? "And what—he wants you to go with him?"

"Well, he told me I was welcome. I could make some money. For us. And do something good. Maybe we could even sell some at your shop."

She felt sick, not because Ayoub was thinking of going to

Pakistan, but because whatever he was thinking, she was, or felt herself to be, totally shut out from it. All the people who'd ever said or implied that their marriage was unwise were gathered at the foot of their bed, it now seemed, and were looking at her with the same look on all of their faces: *See?* Her marriage, reflected in their eyes, was thin and ridiculous: an unlucky intersection of delusions they'd happened to hold about themselves when they happened to meet, and that they'd mistaken for a shared current of magical energy that would run between them forever, making anything possible. But something had gone wrong. The sense of possibility Ayoub had once attached to her he was now obviously eager to attach to something else. She felt like she'd woken up outside in the middle of the night not knowing where she was, just that it was dark and cold.

BRADLEY

He spends most of the drive to the dormer-windows, backyard-pool house in Benson thinking maybe he shouldn't be going. Maybe he should be pulling over, calling Melanie, explaining the whole thing. Or having his secretary call her and say that Chaz Benedict sends his apologies but won't be able to make it. (How his secretary came up with Chaz Benedict he can't begin to imagine: it sounds like the name of a spy from an old porno.) Or maybe the thing to do is just not show and let that be that. She would never know.

But they need to talk. It's been almost seven full days. He deserves to know what's happening. Does Art know? Could Sheri find out? For half the week this possibility has felt unthinkably far away, so far it could never harm him; for the other half it has been a swarm of insects coming to devour everything he knows. From hour to hour, and sometimes even minute to minute, he's swung from one to the other: far away; close; no problem; swarm of insects.

For now, Sheri obviously has no idea, a fact that is the source of great relief—and also pain. A reminder of the trust he violated.

He keeps the radio off. He hasn't listened to music all week. At the Benson house, Melanie's gray Civic is in the driveway. Someone should tell her that if she's trying to sell houses like this one—nicer, more expensive houses—she needs a new car. No one with enough money to buy this house will be convinced to do so by a woman driving a gray Civic.

The front door is unlocked. Walking in, he hears her in the kitchen, muttering to herself as she fiddles with the microwave or the oven; something that beeps. It's a nice house, and it's obvious that no one is living there. Everything is too clean, too exactly in its right place.

"Is that you, Chaz?" she calls out in a funny meeting-a-stranger voice he hasn't heard before. "I'm in the kitchen!" He doesn't know what to do with the fact that, no matter how much he wishes none of it had ever happened, there seems to be some part of him that, hearing her voice, is wondering whether, now that they are alone together, they will end up having sex.

Sex in a stranger's house in showing-for-sale condition: it sounds like sex in a hotel, but stripped of that generic hotel sadness.

At this point, would there be any harm in one more time?

This isn't how he should be thinking. Not if he wants to hold on to what's good in his life.

But still: her voice.

The look on her face when she sees him is terrifying: "What are you doing here?" Her eyes move nervously around the kitchen, like she's looking for a path she can use to get past him and flee.

"I'm Chaz Benedict!" He sees the joke isn't landing, but tries to help it along with a nice big grin. There's maybe fifteen feet of kitchen between them, and much of that space is occupied by a giant island with what appears to be two full stovetops. On the side of the island closest to him, the marble top extends beyond the base, forming a counter with a row of wooden stools underneath.

"What are you doing here?" she says again.

"It was a joke," he says. "From before. But then I thought—"

"A joke?"

"I thought we could—"

"What's the joke? Using a fake name to trick me into meeting you in an empty house? Is that the joke?"

"Oh, come on. Look, I said this was before what happened. But we need to talk."

"If you have something to tell me, send me a letter. Or write me an email. This is inappropriate. This is bizarre."

"We need—"

"There is no 'we.' It's over."

"It was a joke!" He has no problem with someone not finding a joke funny. It happens. Everyone has a right to an opinion. But there is something obtuse—something combative—about refusing to even acknowledge a joke as a joke. To treat it like something else. The look on her face reminds him of college: how when some girls ran into old boyfriends in the hallway or on the quad, they would pretend not just that they didn't like the old boyfriends *now* but that they had in fact *always* disliked them.

"Please leave." She folds her arms in front of her chest. "Now."

"We need to talk, Melanie. What's going on with Michael?"

"We're not talking about Michael. We're talking about you leaving. You're leaving. This is insane."

"But we're here now, so—"

"Leave. Just leave."

"You know," he says. "It takes two to tango."

"Please leave."

"Jesus Christ, Melanie." He turns and does what she asks. He's back in the driveway, just a few feet away from his truck—Michael's scratches are still there, ruining the perfection of the surface; he's been too busy to take it to the shop—when he hears the front door of the house open behind him.

"Bradley!"

His first instinct is to keep going. Get in his truck, close the door—not slam it, he's not a cliché—and drive off. But he stops himself and turns around. "What?"

"I know," she says. She bites her lip. He's never seen her bite her lip before. He has to admit there's something charming about it.

"Know what?"

She closes her eyes. Takes a deep breath. "Nothing. Or . . . not nothing. I know it takes two to tango. Like you said. I know this isn't just your fault."

"Thank you," he says. "Thank you for saying that. Should we go inside and talk?"

And then her face changes and he's a criminal again, a criminal who has just suggested that at the next school board meeting they should fuck onstage for laughs. "There's nothing to talk about," she says. "Now. Please go."

Getting into his truck, he tries to restrain himself from slamming the door. He succeeds. He resolves not to look in his rearview mirror, but forgets, then wonders whether she can tell—whether she can see him looking back at her. And then it doesn't matter: he's too far away, and even if he weren't, he isn't looking anymore. He turns the radio back on. He puts the volume up, loud.

He calls his office and says he'll be back later than expected. Instead of heading back to town, he heads to the Paradise

Grove Mall. There, in the jewelry store on the second floor of the east wing, he buys Sheri a silver necklace, one he knows she wants because that morning, scouring the kitchen for his keys, he found a picture of it she'd clipped from a magazine.

Watching the clerk box the necklace, he feels his pulse ticking up, sweat forming on his neck, his back. The necklace is for his wife, so why does he feel just as self-conscious as if he were buying it for Melanie? He's never bought her anything besides wine, which hardly counted—they both drank it. No lingerie, no jewelry, no shoes: nothing that said *a present for my partner in cheating*. A convenient way, he is now forced to admit, for him to avoid acknowledging a simple truth of their relationship: that whatever else they are—or were—they are also cheaters.

"Oh my," says Sheri. "Wow."

"You like it?"

"What's the occasion?"

"Who says I need an occasion? It's for you. To celebrate you." He means it. He knows he also bought the necklace for other reasons—for himself, essentially—but he doesn't think this truth is mutually exclusive with the truth that he bought it because he loves his wife. As she takes the necklace out of its box and tries it on, shaking her neck and shoulders to make sure it settles where it's going to settle, he gets to see multiple eras of her good looks playing like a flipbook— flipping now forward, now back—across her face, together forming one beautiful expression of surprised delight.

"I actually had my eye on this one," she says.

"I know." He explains: his lost keys, her desk, the clipping. Her face darkens.

"What's wrong?" he says.

"Nothing—but you know, I didn't put it there so you would—"

"Of course not."

"I wasn't trying—"

"No, no."

"I would hate it if you thought—"

"No, I was just looking for my keys."

"You promise?"

"Of course I promise. I can't even imagine you thinking like that. Come on." He starts humming, improvising something like a waltz, humming louder and louder. He grabs his wife and dances her around the kitchen, fast enough and for long enough that when they stop they're breathing hard.

"Well," she says. "Thank you."

Later, in bed, she comes to him. "I want you," she whispers, smearing the words into his shoulder. He should be pleased: Isn't this what he told her he was missing? It doesn't come naturally to her—he knows that. And yet here she is, trying.

He is unhappy to discover that he can't stop himself from wondering about the extent to which it's a performance. They made love for the first time when they were eighteen, moving gently on a pile of blankets in the bed of his truck. He'd never been so happy. What changed? Was it a million little changes, or one big change, and was there really any difference? The immediate problem is the necklace, he tells himself. The necklace makes him feel like he's paying for it, like she's working for her prize, and while he knows that feeling does it for some people, he doesn't count himself among them. He regrets buying it. He's glad when it's over, and stays awake for a long time afterward, becoming every minute more attuned to tiny variations in the near stillness of the night. A rustling branch. A car's engine humming, the rubber of its tires on the road. His wife, beside him, breathing in and breathing out.

AMIRA

The landlord's son's flashy little red Fiat is parked in front of the office, so she turns and heads to the post office instead. Half an hour later the Fiat's still there, so she turns away again and heads to the market. After the market, the car is still there. She has no choice. The rent is due.

"Signora!" He makes a show of looking at his watch. "I was wondering if I'd be seeing you today."

She forces herself to smile. "Here I am."

"You're well?"

"Yes, thank you." She reaches into her purse for the rent envelope.

"And your husband?"

"He's well, thank you."

"I don't see him around."

"No?"

"No."

She holds out the rent envelope and he takes it.

"It must be a relief to have him back, though."

"Of course, yes."

"But I don't see him at the butcher's."

"No."

"He's working somewhere else?"

"He's still deciding," she says. "People have been wonderful. Lots of opportunities." A lie hardly counts when you're talking to a person like the landlord's son.

"Ah, well. That's good. Of course, he's been through a lot, hasn't he?"

"Yes."

"But it's good to have options. Let me tell you, as a businessman: options are a good thing to have. Will you tell him I say hello?"

"I will." Never again, she resolves, will she risk having to hand the rent to the landlord's son in person. She will come only at night, after work, and slide the envelope through the slot.

When she gets home, the door to the spare room is closed. Either he's asleep on the floor, or he's awake and doesn't want to come out. She moves as quietly as possible to the kitchen. She has the ingredients for a few possible dinners—and no idea which one to make. She no longer has a firm sense of what he likes. Neither, it seems, does he. Even if something appeals to him on a shopping day, this is no guarantee that it will appeal to him later. A dish might get his appetite going at dinnertime, but this is no guarantee that, shortly after eating it, he won't be in the bathroom feeling sick. In the first days of his return, he ate only five or six bites total of the tonnarelli alla Ayoub she made with Meryem and Nada. She had to throw the rest away; the idea of eating it herself was too painful. She made it again a few weeks later, and that time he devoured a whole bowl. Watching from across the table, she felt concerned by how quickly he was moving the food from the world into his body, but this concern was washed away by a fierce tide of relief so strong it almost made her cry. It wasn't long, though, before he dashed to the bathroom. After he'd been inside for ten minutes, she asked through the door if he was okay. He said he was fine. At the twenty-five-minute mark she felt the first pinprick signs that she had to pee soon. At the thirty-minute mark she started pondering the mechanics of pissing in the kitchen sink. In the end it didn't come to that, but ever since she has used the bathroom more often, whether or not she feels the urge.

A month later, on a Sunday, getting food ready for the week, she asked him if they should have tonnarelli alla Ayoub for dinner. He said yes. The next day he sent her a text while she was at work, the first one he'd sent her since his return: *looking forward to TAA dinner.* When she got home, he told her that he wasn't feeling well enough to eat. "I'm sorry, sweet one," he said. "Can you put some in the fridge? I'll eat it tomorrow."

For the rest of the week she had tonnarelli alla Ayoub for lunch at work. Eating it was just as demoralizing as she'd anticipated; Ayoub never ended up having any. But she had no choice: she—they—couldn't afford to throw food away.

He comes out of the spare room rubbing his eyes. "You're home." He says it in Italian; it's almost always Italian now. Her Arabic will never recover, never improve.

"Do you want dinner?" This is better, she has decided—more open, less confining—than *What do you want for dinner?*

His head ticks slightly from side to side while he thinks. "Maybe just some fruit." He always wants fruit now. She has made herself an expert in the evaluation of bruised fruit, partially discolored fruit, almost but not quite overripe fruit. She goes to the market later in the day, hoping for discounts on fruit that Walid and the other vendors have failed to sell. Sometimes Ayoub comes with her to identify what looks good to him. But the crowds make him nervous, and her awareness of his nervousness makes it difficult to bargain hunt as effectively as possible, and so she often goes alone.

Two pears for him, bean stew for her. Pear juice drips down his beard, onto his lap. Beads of pear juice sit on his bushy beard. She thinks about telling him but decides not to. He never had a beard before, and she's still surprised he hasn't shaved it off, to banish the reminder of where he was and what he went through. He finishes his second pear. He asks if there's another. "Yes, two more." She holds herself back from recommending that he not eat any more pears tonight, or at least not right away. He eats a third pear, then a fourth. While she does the dishes, he sits with her in the kitchen. No bathroom run needed. It's good, she tells herself, to have him sitting there while she washes dishes. It's important, she tells herself, to name the good things as they come.

She has been forced to modify her bedtime routine.

They pray Isha together, the way they used to. (Ayoub does all five prayers now—not, he says, because he feels any more religious or devout, but because he's "used to it.")

If he's still awake when she gets into bed—and he usually is—she leaves on whatever lights are already on.

If he's gone into the spare room, she leaves on the small lamp in the living room, plus the kitchen lights at the lowest setting the dimmer will allow.

If it seems he's going to attempt to spend the night in bed with her, she turns off all the lights.

She can't name any logic behind this system; it's just her system.

She likes the idea of sleeping together with her husband, of course she does, but on nights when he joins her in bed, she lies awake in effortful awareness of the fact that he isn't sleeping, and that he knows she's awake, and that he knows it's because of him. She taught him some of Sarah's breathing exercises, and sometimes she hears him trying to use them. She's usually still awake—even if she's pretending not to be—when he leaves the bed and heads to the spare room.

Tuesdays are no longer built around wandering the city. She misses the walks, how they structured not just Tuesdays but the entire week, draining her energy, emptying her mind, helping her sleep. But he walks so slowly now and can't go far without his back protesting. He doesn't like being away from their bathroom. He gets tired. She wants to walk and walk and walk—but doesn't want to leave him when they could be together. Someday, she tells herself, things will be different.

One Tuesday morning they're sitting at the kitchen table and he asks if she remembers how they used to take the bus to the Appian Way Park.

"Of course I remember."

"Should we go?"

"Today?"

"When else?" She can see him enjoying her surprise. She's learned so much, in the months since his return, about the danger of putting too much weight—any weight, really—on anything: any one meal, any one conversation, the mood or feel of any individual hour. Name the good things, yes. But don't take them as signs that anything is getting better (or getting worse). She knows this. And yet, packing her bag for the Appian Way Park, she cannot completely stave off a little rush of happiness.

The hard seat of the bus gives him back trouble, and in the open grassy section of the park he looks afraid, like he thinks the sky might vacuum him up. On the tree-lined paths he seems claustrophobic and worried about who might be coming around the next bend. She hasn't told him what it was like to come here by herself: about convincing herself that she could feel his presence in the trees; about telling Sarah; about learning that this was, apparently, a common experience.

On the way back to the bus, they pass their beloved coffee bar. She wants the owner to spot them and call them over, all happy surprise, cappuccinos on the house. But it doesn't happen. She can't remember the last time she saw the owner; for all she knows he is dead or retired.

"Do you want a coffee?" he says. In the week after he came back, he drank maybe half a dozen coffees before accepting they upset his stomach too much. "We can sit if you like. I'll just have water. I can still enjoy the smell, probably."

She understands he's trying to be nice. But as bad as it feels to say no, she knows that saying yes—actually sitting and drinking a cappuccino while he drinks water and watches and says he enjoys the smell (or confesses that it bothers him)—will feel worse.

"Let's go home," she says, and they do.

. . .

In the foyer, she sees through the slot in the front of the mailbox that something's been delivered. She thinks she recognizes the familiar texture and padding of a Red Cross envelope.

Which it can't be.

But it is.

"What's that? Give it to me." Grabbing it from her is the most physically forceful thing she's seen him do since he came back. She's about to reflexively apologize—for what?—but he's already climbing the stairs, his right leg doing most of the work, lunging up and planting down and heaving the rest of him along. He has his own key, and by the time she gets to the apartment he's in the spare room. The room that would be their child's room if they had a child. The door is closed. She calls his name. No response. She calls it again. "Say something. Talk to me."

The door opens and he comes out. "Show me. The other letters. Now. Please."

The day she found out he was coming back, after she showed the letters to Meryem, she moved the shoebox to the bottom drawer of her bedroom dresser, behind some old sweatpants. She goes to the bedroom, retrieves it, and brings it to the living room; before she can hand it to Ayoub, he reaches out and grabs it. She tries to tell him with her eyes that he's frightening her, but he doesn't notice, or he notices and doesn't care, or he notices and cares but not enough to act differently. He scurries back to the spare room. Shuts himself in.

"Ayoub?" She keeps her distance from the door in case he comes flying out.

"Not now."

"Fine." She goes into the bedroom, slams the door, and hurls herself onto the bed. She tells herself she might stay there for the rest of the day, through the night, until tomorrow. Or maybe she'll just leave. Go walking. *I'M GOING OUT!* she could call out as she left. *I DON'T KNOW WHEN I'LL BE BACK!*

His voice comes from the hallway. She must not have heard him leave his room. "Amira?"

"What?"

"Are there others?"

"Other what?"

"Did you give me all the letters?"

"Yes."

"Do you promise?"

"I'm not lying."

"I didn't say you were lying."

"Okay."

"I just wanted to know."

She stays on the bed and somehow falls asleep. She hasn't slept during the day since before Ayoub went missing, out of a vague fear that doing so would be the first step toward the dissolution of the routines that held her life together. When she wakes, the room is dark. She can't remember dreaming. She moves groggily to the kitchen. Ayoub's there, and as soon as he sees her, he's up from his chair, apologizing for what he did, how he acted, the way he spoke to her. According to the clock above the oven, it's two in the morning.

"It's okay, Ayoub," she says.

"No, it's not."

"They were always coming late. Out of order."

"I see."

He sits back down. He stands back up. He asks if she's hungry, if he can get her something from the fridge. Something to drink? He was about to make himself some more tea— does she want tea?

"I should probably just sleep." His face falls a little. "But— okay, one tea. Decaf."

"Of course decaf. It's the middle of the night."

She watches him put the kettle on for her, take down a cup and saucer for her, pick a decaf tea bag for her, pour the boiling water into the cup for her. They sit and sip. She's glad she accepted his offer. The cats start shrieking in the alley, and she asks if this is their first fight of the night. He nods. Talking about the cat noises has become for them something like talking about the weather. Every little development gets discussed, or at least noted. Like her, he doesn't remember ever hearing the cats before his time away.

"Is the tea good?"

"It's perfect."

The room fills up with that middle-of-the-night feeling. The world outside might not exist. It's a feeling with a good version and a bad version, and it's been too long since she touched the good one.

* * *

After work the next day, she stops to check her email. She doesn't use the Somali cafe anymore. The new place she goes to is bland and less friendly—there's no tea, you pay at the beginning instead of when you're done—but it has no associations with Ayoub's absence. She hardly gets any messages. Sarah sends updates about the progress—or not—of various lawsuits she's filed on Ayoub's behalf, and occasional clues she's uncovered about what happened to Arsalan. (Just once, she made herself stop by the pizza counter to see if anyone there knew anything; no one did, or at least no one told her anything.) Mourad asks for updates, hungry to know more than the little Ayoub seems to tell him on the phone; he offers to send money, he wishes her well, he sends pictures of his family. Besides those two, she has no regular correspondents.

Today she has just one new email, from Sarah. It contains an article—translated into Italian by her office—about how, in Morocco, a government commission has finally begun gathering testimonies from people formerly held and tortured in the country's secret prisons, with the official aim of dispelling secrecy on the subject and deciding on appropriate compensation for victims and their families. Sarah has written to her about this commission before. At first, it felt exciting: she assumed that telling the truth about secret prisons would, eventually, mean telling the truth about Ayoub. But then she learned that, by law, this commission was forbidden to look into any cases more recent than 1999. Certainly they wouldn't touch anything the government had done in collaboration with America. *I know it is disappointment,* Sarah wrote, *but each small bricks is building the wall.* She wishes

Sarah would stop emailing her about the commission, but doesn't like the idea of asking her not to.

She sees the email went to Ayoub (who has never said a thing to her about secret prisons in Morocco or anywhere else). But he won't see it; since coming back, he's shown no interest in using the web. He talks to Mourad on the phone, and that seems to be enough. When she tells him about Sarah's lawsuit updates, he listens but has nothing to say. When a translator employed by Sarah's firm sent a letter from a woman in North Carolina explaining her protest group, and asking if she and Ayoub wanted to "tell their story" for their website and flyers, she told him about it and he shook his head.

She has no more emails to deal with, but she stays at the computer for the remainder of the time she's paid for. She can admit to herself that, as often as not, she goes to the new web cafe not because she truly needs or even wants to check her email, but because she wants an excuse to be alone for a moment.

She catches the bus home, but gets off one stop early to extend her walking time. Turning onto their street, she sees a thin, bearded man sitting on a small stool in front of their building. As she gets closer, she sees that the stool is actually an upside-down produce crate, and the thin, stooped man is her husband, stroking the neck of a painfully thin cat that is either covered in street dust or has fur that is the color of street dust, or both. She is forced to ask herself: If the man hadn't been Ayoub, would she have classified him as a flat man? When he sees her coming, he waves with his right hand, keeping his left on the cat.

"Where'd you get that?" she says.

He shrugs like a child with a secret. "She just walked up to me."

"The crate, I mean."

"From Walid."

"You went to the market?"

"I went to the market."

"He sold it to you?" Every Sunday she gives him a small allowance—a few euros, whatever she can spare—so he has some money to spend however he wants. Of course, she gave him an allowance before, too, when he worked at the butcher's. But this is different. She hates it. She sets the money on the kitchen table before she leaves for work to avoid making it a face-to-face interaction.

"I bought some oranges," he says. "Walid gave me the crate for free." The dusty (or dust-colored) cat purrs under his touch, arching its body to tell him it wants more.

"Don't let it bite you!"

"It's a she."

"Well, don't let *her* bite you."

"She won't."

"It probably hasn't had any shots."

"Look." He puts his hand right up against the cat's face, almost inserting it into the creature's mouth, and all it does is lick—quick, greedy licks, one after the other, like Ayoub's hand is the best thing it's ever tasted, and if it doesn't lick all the flavor up now, some other cat might come steal it away.

"Are you hungry?" she says.

"Probably."

"Well, come up soon, then. And make sure you wash your hands. I'm allergic, remember?"

"Of course I remember. I'll just stay for the mail." He points down the street, at the mailman and his cart.

She's in the kitchen for just a few minutes before he walks in, cradling the grocery crate in his arms.

"No mail?"

He shakes his head.

"Don't forget to wash."

"I will, I will." He walks to the sink and starts soaping his hands.

"Said goodbye to your new friend?"

"Yep." He smiles wistfully, as if she asked him not about a cat but about a beloved family member who, until this afternoon, he hadn't seen in years. "I didn't have any food for her, so she moved on. She reminds me . . ."

"Of what?"

"She reminds me of a cat that used to come around our house. My parents' house."

He turns the faucet off and starts toweling his hands. She thinks maybe he's about to elaborate on this cat from his past. He's headed that way, she's sure of it. But something stops him on the way. Maybe, she thinks, it's too painful to think or talk about himself as a child, knowing what awaits this child—himself—in his future. He folds the towel, puts it back on the hanger, and says he probably isn't hungry after all, that he's going to go lie down and might fall asleep. "Okay," she says, and when he's gone, she opens the fridge to see what's there. Something she can heat up. Something easy.

In the morning, she feels hungry and tries to remember what she ended up eating. But she can't. She can't even remember if she ate anything at all.

* * *

"What does he do all day?" says Meryem, who once or twice a week joins her on her walk to work, bringing Nada along in a stroller. "I don't mean that in a rude way."

"Well, he's still getting his strength back. He does things around the house. He cooks. Does the shopping sometimes. Works on his cases."

"His court cases?"

"Exactly."

"Will he work again? I mean, work for money?"

"I don't know. I think so."

"Is it physical, or mental?"

"It's both, Meryem."

"Of course. I didn't mean—"

"I know."

"I didn't mean—"

"It's fine."

"And I'm sure he'll work again," Meryem says. "God willing. In time. That's what it takes, doesn't it? Time?"

A few blocks before Monti they hug goodbye. Hugs from Meryem are still the best hugs she gets. It's good to hug Ayoub, of course, but he's so much thinner and weaker feeling than before, she worries about hurting him, she's more ginger than she has to be, she's too self-conscious for anything like their old hugs. She doesn't want to miss them but she does. She can't help it.

* * *

After work on Saturday, she rides the bus home. When she's two stops away, she takes out her phone and calls Meryem's taxi driver cousin. He doesn't pick up but sends a message right away: *coming!*

Before, whenever they went to Avezzano together, she headed straight to Termini station from work and Ayoub met her there, bringing their bags with him on the bus. But that would be too much for him now, or at least she assumed it would. She didn't ask, afraid that he would feel pressure to put on a brave face, or shame because he couldn't. Instead, she just told him she would call a taxi.

Meryem assured her that her cousin would give them a "family discount," but this hardly feels guaranteed. Anyway, how much is a family discount? For the last month she's been saving up: no coffees, cheaper groceries, fewer bus rides.

The cousin turns out to be incredibly friendly: he acts like he's their personal valet, carrying their bags to the trunk, opening their doors, asking if they want the air hotter or colder, the windows up or down, this or that type of music on the radio. Ayoub hasn't been in a car since the day when she and a lawyer from Sarah's firm met him at the airport in a luxury sedan. She remembers the seats. Creamy leather. She wonders if the cousin treats all his passengers this way, or if he's treating them so nicely because of whatever Meryem told him about Ayoub. Dropping them at the station, he refuses payment altogether. "Please," he says. "If Meryem finds out I took your money, I won't live long enough to spend it."

. . .

Her father is waiting in the train station, holding up a hand-written sign: SIGNOR AND SIGNORA ALAMI. He used to do the same thing when she was a child; she and her mother would go into Rome in the morning and he would pick them up at night, holding a sign, pretending to be their chauffeur. It's sweet. He hasn't seen Ayoub since before, and she watches him attempt to conceal his shock at his son-in-law's changed appearance, watches him deciding how firmly to shake his hand, whether to draw him into a hug, and what kind of hug, and for how long.

The first time she brought Ayoub home, her mother spent the weekend in an endless swirl of activity and small talk that obviously functioned as a shield, protecting her from contact with the basic fact that her daughter had fallen in love with an Arab, a Muslim—to her, the two words were synonyms. Now something similar happens: when they arrive, she's still cooking, but insists they sit at the kitchen table "so we can all be together." The excuse of working on dinner lets her pepper them with question after question—about the journey, about whether the train was crowded, about the condition of both stations, whether they were properly cleaned—without ever being forced to make extended eye contact with either of them. At any moment she has the option of turning back to the stovetop or peering into the oven or going off searching for something deep in a cabinet, in the fridge, in the pantry.

During their negotiations over the visit, Amira made her mother promise two things. First: that she would refrain from pushing food on Ayoub, or from saying anything at all about how much he ate or didn't eat, the amount of time he spent in the bathroom, anything at all related to consumption or digestion. Second: that neither she nor her father would ask any questions or make any reference—however oblique or well intentioned—to Temara or his experience there. ("It's not something he wants to go around talking about," she said. "Can you understand that?") When they eat, her mother follows the second rule completely, but the first only in a narrow, technical sense, pushing food so insistently on Amira and her father that it becomes painfully obvious she isn't pushing any on Ayoub—who, to Amira's surprise, eats more than she's seen him eat in months, trying almost everything her mother has prepared and complimenting her on each dish individually. She wants to urge him to slow down or eat less, but she doesn't want to give her mother the pleasure of seeing her violate her own rule, and so she just sits there, sure that any moment now he'll get up and run to the bathroom.

That first weekend visit with Ayoub, when they were finally alone in her bedroom, she felt suddenly swamped with guilt. She saw, looking back on the evening, that without meaning to or realizing it, she had focused so intently on her parents' responses that she lost sight of him entirely. She started apologizing, trying to explain. They had already, by then, decided to marry, but this was the moment when she began to realize what the idea actually meant to her. "I can't lose sight of you," she said. "I can't. I'm sorry." Ayoub told her not to worry, it was fine, he knew how complicated family could be, they all had plenty of time to figure it out, they were just getting started.

Tonight, they lie on their backs on the full-sized bed she got for her fifteenth birthday, after a year of begging; she can't remember why fifteen-year-old Maria wanted it so much, only the force of the wanting. She and Ayoub haven't discussed their sleeping arrangements for the night, any more than they have ever discussed their sleeping arrangements at home, let alone the fact that since his return they have not made love once. The sex they once had feels almost as distant as the sex she had with Paolo when she was eighteen: a memory, encased firmly in the past. But maybe tonight is different; there's a teenage uncertainty in the air about where their bodies are in relationship to each other. Unless she's just imagining. She feels young. She feels old. She keeps her eyes on the ceiling. "Do you remember the first time I brought you here?" she asks.

He doesn't answer right away.

Maybe he won't answer at all.

"You mean your mom spying on us?"

She wants to hear him tell the story—to be next to him in bed while he reaches back in time, grabs the thread of their life, and stitches it forward into the present, into now—so she pretends not to remember what he's talking about.

"I had to go to the bathroom in the middle of the night. But I didn't want to wake you up. So I was moving extra slowly, and being as quiet as possible. And it turned out your mom—"

"Oh yeah."

"—was trying to listen to us through the wall. But I was being so quiet she didn't even hear me coming. And she tried to pretend she'd just been refilling her water, but—"

"But she didn't have a water glass."

"Exactly. I actually felt bad. She was so flustered."

"She deserved it. And then what happened?"

Again she already knows the answer. What she wants is to

hear him tell the story: how he came back from the bathroom and told her what had happened, how they laughed as quietly as they could, how that only made it funnier, how, still laughing, they came together and had what was both the quietest and most intense sex they'd ever had, face-to-face on their sides, a position they'd never used before but which afterward became one of their favorites.

"That was it," Ayoub says. "I don't remember anything after that. That's the story."

"So what's it like?" her mother asked once on the phone, a month or two after the wedding.

"What's what like?"

"You know. With an Arab."

"Mother." She knew some women talked about sex with their mothers. But not her.

"They say they're absolutely crazy for it, you know. With European women."

"Who's 'they'?"

"You know. Arabs. Africans."

"No, I mean, who's 'they' who's saying they're 'crazy for it'?"

"I don't know. People!"

Two hours later they're both still awake. She asks what he's thinking about.

"Me?"

"Yes, you."

"I'm thinking of Habiba."

"Who?"

"Habiba."

"Who's Habiba?"

Habiba, he tells her, is the name he's given to his favorite of the neighborhood cats. The scrawny little one. "You know the one. You've met."

"Yes, but I didn't know you named it."

"I told you I did."

"No."

"Yes, I remember, I did."

"I don't think so."

When her alarm wakes her for the dawn prayer, she's alone in bed. She finds Ayoub on the back porch, laying out his prayer rug. "Why didn't you wake me?"

"I didn't know you were interested."

"You know I do them all when I'm here." Said out loud, it sounds pathetic.

With a start like that, she doesn't expect much. And perhaps it's this lack of expectation that, for the first time in months, allows the ritual to succeed and open her and the world up to each other.

When they're done, she gets cups of water from the kitchen and they sit on the couch looking out at the small backyard, watching morning come. "Do you wish I prayed with you every morning?"

"You need your sleep. For work."

"Well, maybe on my days off."

"Only if you want."

It's nice, having a little lawn, a little porch. For a second it's obvious to her that they should find a way to leave Esquilino—leave Rome altogether—and move to Avezzano.

For so long she held on to the apartment so that Ayoub had somewhere familiar to return to. So they could have their life back. But if the task is not to restart their old life but instead make a new one, why Rome? What does Esquilino have to offer them, besides suspicious glances and whispers behind their backs? Maybe in Avezzano it could be different. They could have a porch and a lawn. Life could be something else. Life could be new again.

"Will he go back to work?"

She and her mother are walking into town while her father and Ayoub watch football.

"At some point, yeah."

"It's been a while."

"His entire life was ruined."

"But he can have it back now. He's a free man."

"Technically."

"Does he want to work?"

"He's very involved in his cases. The lawsuits."

"And what good does that do?"

"Do you know there are people in America who went looking and found the actual airport where the plane took off? The one they used to fly him to Morocco? They found the proof. People in the town are furious—they're having protests, they're trying to get people arrested."

"Yes, Amira, but—"

"It is criminal, you know. What they did."

"I want to tell you something," her mother says. "I know we've had difficulties, but I want you to forget about that for a moment and listen. Can you do that?" It's something her own father—Amira's grandfather—told her years ago, she explains, during a rough period early in her own marriage. They were out to lunch—just the two of them, a rarity—when, to her surprise, her father told her, with no introduction or preamble, that if she ever decided that she needed a divorce, she could count on him for any support he was able to give. Divorce was much less common then, her mother reminds her; it was unlikely that her parents knew a single divorced person, and she never would have guessed that her father could accept the idea. "So it was a very meaningful moment between us," she says. "A moment when I really understood his love for me, as a parent. Do you understand?"

"But you didn't get divorced."

"No, obviously."

"I don't want to get divorced."

"I'm not saying you do. I'm saying that, if you did, you'd have my support. I'm saying that you have options. Do you understand? I don't just mean divorce. If you and Ayoub want to move somewhere—I'm not saying Avezzano, necessarily, but if—"

"Why would we want to move?"

"That's just an example."

"We like it in Esquilino."

"I'm not saying you don't. I'm just saying—"

"What? What are you saying?"

"I wasn't trying to make you upset."

They walk toward home in silence. When they pass the house that to her will always be Camilla Russo's parents' house, she asks if Camilla's parents still live there. Her mother says that they do. A few blocks later, they pass Paolo's parents' house. She's never been inside, but of course she knows whose house it is. "And what about Paolo's parents? Still there?" She already knows, from Paolo, that they are.

What she didn't know—what her mother learned just the other day from the gossips at the market, and cheerfully tells her now—is that Paolo's getting married to a girl he met in Rome, one of his coworkers. "Isn't that nice?"

Her father and Ayoub look comfortable together. It's sweet, but also slightly disturbing; Ayoub's comfort looks to her like the comfort of a child, a small child embracing his childishness, nestling into the support arranged for him by adults. He's never been a real football fan but appears to be enjoying himself, maybe because "watching football" is a script that anyone is free to pick up and follow: you watch, moments arise where it's appropriate to say something, to agree with or genially dispute what your fellow watchers say, and everyone (or everyone but the dumbest hooligans) knows it ultimately doesn't matter, which is part of what makes it fun.

At the train station her father slips an envelope in her jacket pocket. On the train she opens it: two fifty-euro notes. Ayoub takes from his pocket an identical envelope and opens it: two fifty-euro notes, which he hands over without a hint of complaint.

Halfway back to Rome she calls Meryem's cousin to confirm their arrival time. Again he picks them up, handles their bag, asks about the radio, the windows, the air.

When they pull up, Ayoub opens his door right away, runs to their building, disappears through the front door. She hasn't seen him cover distance so quickly since he's been back. Is he running to the bathroom? Avoiding any exposure, however brief, to the prying gaze of their neighbors? But a second later, he comes back out and kneels down to work the latch that keeps the door open, making it easier to carry bags in.

"Nice," says Meryem's cousin. "I always forget about those things." He gets out of his car and lights up a cigarette. "Don't tell Meryem, okay? She'll kill me." He says it casually: he's not really worried about getting killed.

* * *

In the morning she finds Ayoub slouched forward at the kitchen table, dark trenches of sleep dug under his eyes. "Did you hear it?" he says. "Did you hear the cats?" Apparently, during the night they went at it in the alley, as usual, but it sounded more violent than ever before; he can't believe she slept through it. His speech moves fast, the words must have been spring-loaded inside him for hours and now they're all shooting out at once, bumping into each other along the way, Italian blending with Arabic almost too fast for her to follow. At one point, he says, the noises were so horrible that he thought about going outside and trying to make the fighting stop. "I should have done it. I should have gone down." The worst part was that after the fighting noises died down, another noise started. At first this other noise was faint and infrequent enough for him to convince himself he was imagining it. But soon it became impossible to deny that he was hearing a cat crying in pain. Again he wanted to go downstairs. He couldn't help imagining the cat was Habiba. Again he talked himself out of it. "What if she's lying dead in the alley? What if she's dead because I was too scared to go down there? What if she's hurt?"

"Only one way to find out." She hears how mean she sounds. But she's just woken up; she needs to shower, make coffee, eat, go to Monti, earn money.

"Right." He looks away. "Don't let me slow you down."

Walking to the bus, she considers ducking into the alley to check if a cat is lying there and, if so, how injured it is, or whether it's alive. Then she could call Ayoub, update him, show him that if he cared, she cared. But she slept poorly last

— 149 —

night—she blames her mother's food—and is already behind schedule. She can't afford to miss the bus. When she gets to the alley, she doesn't stop and look; she keeps walking.

Why, riding the bus to work, does she feel she might cry?

She doesn't want to marry Paolo.

She never wanted to marry Paolo.

She doesn't have a problem with Paolo marrying one of his coworkers—or anyone else.

Of course she doesn't. How could she?

And yet, the news of Paolo's marriage, when she heard it from her mother, threatened to bring tears to her eyes—and now the tears are back, trying to escape again.

She almost told her mother the whole story, if only to have told it to someone and, by doing so, proved that she had nothing to hide. But she knew that once she started, she would cry, and she knew that if she cried, her mother wouldn't really listen, would grab on to the wrong idea and never let it go.

Had his whole romance with his bride-to-be transpired entirely in the last four months? Had they fallen in love so quickly and intensely that they simply had to marry right away?

Or was it already happening while she and Paolo were meeting and talking?

If so, why did he never once mention it?

This would, of course, have been "allowed."

Their relationship wasn't romantic; there were no rules; there was no contract. They had been—they were—old friends who made love a few times when they were eighteen and who, more recently, enjoyed talking with each other.

She should have told Ayoub from the start, in the earliest days of his return. *I have something to tell you. It was difficult while you were away. Not as difficult, of course, as it was for you. But difficult. I reconnected with someone from my youth, someone I made love with more than once when we were both eighteen. He turned out to be someone I could talk to. We sat on benches in Monti and talked. He brought me food from the restaurant where he was working—I don't know if he's still working there. And that was it. I thought about not telling you, but I didn't want you to think I had anything to hide. I can imagine how it might look, to some people, but it wasn't like that.*

For the first time in a long time, she spends the work shift fretting that Paolo might show up. Why would he? She can't explain, not even to herself. She wonders whether his fiancée's heard about her—and, if so, what. Walking home, she pushes her feet hard into the ground, as if by doing so she might grind these thoughts out of existence and be done with them.

At home, she's about to put her key in the lock when she hears someone singing inside. Ayoub. She presses her ear to the door. She doesn't recognize the melody but instantly enjoys it: like all her favorite songs, it sounds like it's marking an ending and a beginning at the same time. It doesn't seem to have words, but maybe it does and she can't hear them through the door. Twice the singing stops, then, after a few seconds, starts again. After the third stop, there's a longer pause, like maybe he senses someone's at the door.

She puts her key in the lock and calls out a hello.

He's sitting cross-legged on the floor with his back against the couch, and his eyes are alternating between her and the patch of floor immediately in front of him, where there's a towel with something on it, something alive and dust colored with bloody scrapes and smears all over; it should be obvious what it is but her brain won't tell her. She keeps looking, and by continuing to look, she starts to understand.

It's the cat.

It feels wrong to just stand by the stove getting dinner ready like usual. Like what's happened is fine. But she can't make out the path from saying nothing to saying what she feels.

"I know I should have called," he says. "But I didn't want to bother you at work."

Before they eat, she goes to the bathroom to get an allergy pill. Once she's there, she realizes she's forgotten her water; rather than taking the pill to the kitchen and pouring a glass, she forces it down her throat dry. As soon as they sit down, Ayoub starts lathering her with compliments: the food looks so good, thank you for making it, he didn't know where he'd be without her, he wants to start contributing more to the household . . . Every thirty seconds or so he tilts his chair back and peeks in the living room.

"Should we go eat out there? So we can be closer to your friend?" She regrets how caustic her sarcasm sounds and is about to open her mouth to apologize—but Ayoub speaks first.

"Really?" he says. "Can we?"

They sit on the couch with their plates and watch the cat like it's TV. It keeps lifting its head like it wants to watch them back, but each time the lifting takes more energy than it has and right away its head falls, triggering a full-body shudder that, to judge from the look on Ayoub's face, is the most fascinating thing he's ever seen. He's so absorbed in watching the animal's every move that he doesn't seem to notice that his wife finds the creature's presence in their apartment repulsive.

"I'm allergic," she says. "Remember?"

"But you have pills for that."

"Yes. I took one." She has a sore spot in her throat from swallowing it dry.

"I should try cleaning her again." He takes his plate away and comes back with some towels and their bottle of disinfectant. Sitting cross-legged on the floor, he dabs carefully at each scrape and cut; it's obvious the cat finds it uncomfortable, but it doesn't have enough energy to do much other than mewl and swipe in slow motion in Ayoub's direction. He tsk-tsks and makes soft little murmurings about how it has to stay still, how he's *doing this for your own good, sweet one*. When the cat gets interested in his fingers, he starts using one of them as a lure, moving the cat's gaze around as a distraction while he inspects more of its body.

"I don't really know what I'm doing." He says it so softly that at first she thinks he's murmuring more comfort to the cat. But even though he's looking at the cat he's talking to her; he doesn't know how to properly clean an animal's wounds, he says, and he's hoping that she will help him get Habiba to a veterinarian's office in the morning. He knows money is tight, he says, but he's been holding on to some of his allowance, so he can help. Plus, he's more than willing to take a lower allowance in the future. Even no allowance.

She knows nothing about veterinarians, let alone the transportation of cats to veterinary appointments. She calls Meryem and right away can hear in her voice that she finds the whole thing exciting. Meryem doesn't know anything about veterinarians, either, but suggests getting in touch with Bouchra, who has four or five cats.

"I don't think Bouchra likes me," Amira says.

"Don't be silly. Why not?"

"At Nada's birthday party she gave me a death stare."

"That's just her face."

"I know her face. It wasn't just her face."

"She loves cats, though."

"What if I don't want help from someone who gives me death stares?"

"Just think of it as coming from me. She's going to help me, I'm going to help you."

Fifteen minutes later Meryem calls back, sounding even more excited. Bouchra was thrilled to help, she says: not only did she recommend an affordable veterinary clinic in Pigneto, but she also offered to loan them a cat carrier. "I'll go pick it up now, then bring it over in the morning." She's already called her cousin, and he's agreed to drive them to and from the clinic.

That night she sleeps horribly. Ayoub spends the night in the living room, on the couch with the cat on the floor in front of him, and she hears every little noise they make. She closes her eyes and does some of Sarah's breathing exercises. She tries to imagine herself walking—tries to re-create an imaginary walk through the city, the interplay of storefronts and doorways and people and signs and weather and her own body, all in motion, separately and together. And then it's morning. Meryem's texting: *on my way!* Ayoub's cleaning the cat again, cooing over it like it's a human baby. When Meryem gets there, she joins in. "I think it's wonderful," she says. "I think it's a wonderful thing to help a suffering animal."

"Thank you," says Ayoub.

"Really. I mean it."

"The trouble is, I'm allergic," says Amira.

Meryem frowns. "But there are pills for that, right?"

On the few times her friend has come over since Ayoub's been back, the two of them have obviously not known what to do with the other, giving their interactions a painful awkwardness, all the more painful because, before, they'd known each other well. But now she sits with Ayoub on the couch and eagerly receives a guided tour of all the cat's wounds, a summary of its behavioral patterns, its "cute" quirks.

In Meryem's cousin's taxi they sit in the back with the carrier between them. The vet is actually a bit east of Pigneto, farther than Meryem said. "I hope this isn't affecting your workday too much," Amira says.

"No, no," the cousin says. "Please."

The vet is a cheerful young man with a calm, competent manner and an extraordinarily good haircut. How wonderful for him, thinks Amira—genuine admiration and bitterness seeping together—to have identified a career that he loved; to have received the training he needed; to have found his way to opening a cozy little business of his own where he can go each day and do what he does best, making money he can use to pay for excellent haircuts.

"Whoever cleaned these," he says, inspecting the cat's wounds, "could come and have a job here. Fantastic work." Ayoub puffs with pride. The vet takes out a flashlight and starts peering into one of the cat's ears. "Now tell me. Are you looking to keep this kitty at home with you?"

They answer at the exact same time, her *No* and Ayoub's *Yes* splotching together in the air between them. The vet says nothing, just switches his flashlight to the other ear. *All part of the job*, she imagines him thinking. *All part of the job.*

"The thing is, we can't really have a cat," she says. "I'm allergic."

"But we have the pills," says Ayoub.

"Well, the pills don't work for everyone," the vet says, casting her a quick glance that seems designed to let her know that he's on her side, or at least attempting to be a neutral party. "Do you know if they work for you, Amira?"

"As far as I know, they work fine. That doesn't mean I want to take one every day. They're not cheap."

The vet smiles. "It seems you have some things to discuss. Which is completely normal."

Out in the lobby the receptionist informs them that "the doctor" has waived almost all of the fees for the appointment, charging only what it took to cover the cost of the shots and antibiotic wash. The young woman's worshipful tone makes Amira feel that she is being asked to recognize the veterinarian as some kind of hero. She wants to say something unkind, a desire that builds as they are somehow convinced to purchase a bag of cat litter, a plastic litter tray, and a small bag of nutrient-fortified food designed specifically for undernourished cats. There are bigger bags available, which are, the receptionist points out twice, quite a bit more economical in the long run.

"No," she says. "No. The small bag is fine."

Outside, Meryem's cousin is waiting for them, leaning against his car and smoking a cigarette. "Don't tell my cousin. If she knows—"

"She'll kill you, right?" says Ayoub, grinning.

"Exactly, brother. Exactly."

On the drive home they sit in silence with Bouchra's carrier between them. "So you have a new family member?" asks Meryem's cousin.

"Maybe," says Ayoub. "We're not sure." He makes a hopeful face, as if he thinks that recognizing her opposition will win him the reward of having her abandon it. She turns away from him, toward the window, and closes her eyes and sets her mind to the budget, wondering how she will compensate for all the money they've already spent today. When she opens her eyes, she sees that Ayoub is studying a brochure about cat care.

Back at the apartment, she right away goes to the kitchen and starts filling a bucket with hot, soapy water.

"Are we going to talk about it?" says Ayoub.

"Maybe after I get some work done."

"Okay."

She mopped the floors last Sunday, and generally considers mopping an every-other-week chore. But now she mops them again. She cleans the stovetop until it shines. She cleans under the bed. She takes everything out of the fridge, even the shelves, and wipes them down. She wipes down the fridge walls. All the while she hears her husband in the living room playing with his cat, cooing, complimenting it for being such a good patient, such a good traveler.

"Are you almost done?" Ayoub calls out. "You're working too hard."

"I don't know," she says. "I'll be done when I'm done."

MEL

On Saturday—two days after their dinner—Linda emailed to invite them to the first official meeting of the North Carolina Anti-Torture Action Network, to be held on Monday night in the basement of the Raleigh Unitarian Church. An hour later, she called to ask if they'd seen it, and whether they were coming. The group's name, she said, was not yet official, and she hoped it would change. "I mean, it doesn't even spell anything."

They had her on speakerphone, at the kitchen table. "Of course we're coming," said Art.

"Have you seen your guy yet, Melly?"

"Who?" she said, though of course she knew.

"Welk."

"No."

"When will you?"

"I'm not sure, Linda."

"Okay, well, try to think of a new name. For the group. Something that actually spells something."

Sunday they cleaned the house.

On Monday she was at the office, imitating a productive person, when her cell phone buzzed. MICHAEL CELL. She picked up and started walking out to the parking lot.

"Look," he said—no *Hello*, no *Hi, Mom*—"I don't want to know anything about it. Okay? I don't want to know how it happened, or how often it happened, or why, or how you feel about it, or anything. I don't want to know anything."

She'd never heard him talk like this—like something chaotic and rough inside him was getting squeezed through a machine that pressed it into the artificial smoothness of words, grammar, sentences. She wished they were together, face-to-face. She realized what she should have done: driven to Asheville and shown up at his door. Gone to him, in recognition of the fact that he had come to her, even if she still didn't know why.

"Of course," she said. "Whatever you want."

"I talked to Dad yesterday."

"I know."

"It was horrible. It's like I know this thing about him, I know what you did, and he has no idea."

"I'm sorry. I'm sorry, Michael."

"Yeah."

"What can I do?"

"Is it over?"

"Yes," she said. Silence—a thick stretch of it. "Can I ask you a question?"

When he was little, that phrase made him laugh: *That is a question!* he used to shriek, his whole face lighting up with his insight.

"Go ahead," he said.

"That night. Why were you coming home?"

"I don't know. No reason, really."

"No reason?"

"Yeah."

Her first thought was that he was obviously lying—that

he'd lied to her so few times in his life that, when he did, she couldn't miss it. But this thought was quickly replaced by another: that it was possible he'd lied to her many more times than she was aware of and that, in believing otherwise, she'd been flattering herself. Maybe the distance between them now—her sense that she was talking to a stranger—wasn't actually a new development. Maybe she just hadn't noticed it before.

"Are you going to tell Dad?"

"Is that what you want, or what you don't want?"

"You weren't going to?"

"That's not what I said. I asked if that's what you want."

"Yes. That's what I want."

"Then I'll tell him."

"But also, Mom?"

"Yes?"

"Leave me out of it, okay? I don't want him to know I know. Okay?"

"Whatever you want, Michael."

"If he wants me to know, he can tell me. And if he doesn't . . ."

"I understand," she said. "I understand."

"Okay. Good."

"I'm sorry, Michael." Silence. "How are you? How's school?"

"I have to go."

As soon as she and Art were both home from work, they drove to Raleigh, alternating between silence and brainstorming better names for the group and trying to remember the last time they went to the Unitarian church basement.

In the Carlson Street era, more than one group they were involved with gathered there. The Unitarians made it available to whoever needed it: activists, local bands, writing groups. To qualify, you didn't have to be members of the congregation, or even Unitarian at all, though it seemed to help if at least one person from your group could at least plausibly claim to be. There was a list of time slots. You called up the keeper of the list. You picked an available slot. Before your first meeting, you came early and were assigned a drawer in a tall storage cabinet against the wall. You signed a pledge that your group wouldn't damage the place. You got a key for your cabinet drawer. You signed a pledge that said you'd return the key. As a side benefit, you also sometimes picked up a few new members, whether from the congregation or from the groups who used the basement in the time slots right before and right after yours.

Mel thought the last time they were there was for a nukes thing.

Art thought she was right.

Nuclear weapons or nuclear power or both?

They couldn't remember.

The closer they got to the church, the stranger it felt. Standing in the parking lot, she felt she was dreaming. The basement was basically the same. A little scuffed from use, maybe. The storage cabinet had probably been replaced at some point. But the linoleum tiles appeared to be the same linoleum tiles; the fluorescent lights seemed to Mel like the same fluorescent lights, humming the same steady hum. The biggest difference was the age balance of the people there. In Mel's memory, the room skewed young: lots of midtwenties, some thirties, a few forties. Now everyone—all twenty people or so—appeared to be forty or older. Gray or graying hair everywhere. A few people looked vaguely familiar, like maybe they had once marched together, strategized together, debated each other. But she couldn't tell for sure.

When Linda saw they were there, she started leading them around the room from group to group. *Old friends of ours,* she kept saying.

Our oldest friends.

From way back.

The ones I was telling you about.

The ones who live in Springwater.

People's eyes kept lighting up, like they were looking at emissaries from another galaxy who had just disembarked from their space vessels.

She reached for Art's hand and squeezed it and he squeezed back.

The meeting was run by a young lawyer named Ashley from the North Carolina chapter of the ACLU. She talked about how good it was to see so many people gathered on such short notice for such an important cause. "Especially our friends from Springwater." She nodded in their direction; everyone looked. There wasn't much in the way of an introduction; people jumped straight to divvying up assignments, deciding who would research hosting options for a website, who would set up an email list, who would investigate the logistical components—laws, permits, parking spots, and so on—of any eventual protest at the airport. A man named Murph wrote down who signed up for what. People kept saying his name—Murph—but Mel kept forgetting it; he had a bowling ball gut and a long white beard, and each time she looked at him, all she could think was: Santa. It was all moving so fast. She understood, of course, that the purpose of the group wasn't to go slow on her behalf, or Art's—the purpose was to take action.

She and Art accepted two tasks.

First: to write emails—"in your own voice" and "as citizens of Springwater"—to people who had been transported to torture sites by Arcadian flights. In cases where those people were still imprisoned and unable to receive letters, they would write to their spouses or parents. The letters could be written in English, said Ashley (as if they knew any other languages), and would be translated by a service kept on retainer by a New York law firm that represented rendition victims.

Second: to begin drawing up a list of Springwater residents who might be worth approaching about joining their cause.

After the meeting officially adjourned, but before the group dispersed, Mel found her way to Ashley, the lawyer, and tried to ask her, as quickly and quietly as possible, what was actually known for sure about Bradley's involvement. "I'm not trying to let him off the hook," she said. "I'm really not. I just want to know. We're on the school board together, which doesn't mean that—"

"I get it," said Ashley. "Life is complicated."

But then Art, Linda, and Robert walked over and joined them. "What's up?" said Linda, rubbing her hands together like they were sharing good gossip.

"Mel's just wondering about Bradley Welk," said Ashley. "About his exact role."

She felt the heat on her cheeks. Her throat tightening. But she couldn't figure out how to change course. Was it possible, she heard herself asking, that Bradley wasn't actually one of Arcadian's owners? Forging signatures, appropriating identities, setting people up: weren't these exactly the types of activities the CIA was known for? Part of the reason the agency was so objectionable? When she'd posed the questions to herself, in her head, they'd sounded reasonable. But now Art and Linda and Robert were looking at her like she was insane. It had been a tactical error, she realized, not to have shared the questions with Art before. Now it seemed that she'd intentionally kept them from him. But she couldn't stop talking; all she could do was talk faster. Was it possible that Bradley had been duped? That even if he had signed the Arcadian incorporation papers, he'd done so not knowing what it actually meant to do so, or that it had anything to do with torture? What, at this stage, did they really know for sure?

"I think these are reasonable questions," said Ashley. They might learn more, she said, when the *Times* story came out; she knew that Keith had planned to interview Bradley, or at least to try, but she didn't know if it had happened yet. "This is completely between us, of course."

"Of course."

"Melly can keep a secret," said Linda.

"You really think Brad might have been set up?" Art asked on the drive home.

"Oh, I don't know."

"You're worried about the budget?"

"I guess so. Yeah."

"What a mess."

"Did you think the one guy looked like Santa? The guy taking down all the notes?"

"Murph?"

"Murph, yeah. With that beard?"

"I can see it. I was thinking more old-timey train conductor, I guess. Because of the hat."

"What hat?"

"He had a hat."

"What kind?"

"The old-timey-train-conductor kind."

Exiting the highway, he turned the wrong way.

"Where are we going?"

"I've been wanting to see it."

At the airport he pulled into the row of parking spaces closest to the main brick building. How comically small it was, even smaller than she remembered. Probably smaller than their house. On the runway there was a tiny refueling truck with a Shell logo on the tank; just like the airport didn't look like a real airport, the truck didn't look like a real truck. It looked like a toy.

There was just one other car in the lot.

The sky wasn't dark but the sun had set and its light was seeping away.

There was some relationship between the view through their windshield—the little brick building, the toy refueling truck, the grass, the runway, the trees, the beginning of dusk—and the men stacked in pyramids, the man in the hood, the men in orange jumpsuits, everything that had been done to them.

Pulling out of the airport parking lot, Art turned the wrong way.

"What are you doing?"

He quickly turned, onto a small paved road she'd never noticed before. "What are you doing?" she said again. It was dark now, and the little road they were on was framed tightly by trees on either side.

The road, he said, was called Bob Fox Road, and it had just one purpose: giving people access by car to the Arcadian Airlines hangar, which was larger than the other hangars, and considerably farther from the airport. In the beam of their headlights she could see a fence and a guard station, like at a paid parking lot.

"How do you know that?" she said.

"Murph told me."

"Who's Bob Fox?"

"I don't know. It sounds like a military thing. Like Alpha Tango Foxtrot, or whatever. Apparently the hangar is right down there." He flicked the high beams on. "But you can't see it from here. There's a little curve in the road, and it's right after that. That's what Murph said."

"How does Murph know?"

Art flicked the high beams off, then on again. "I don't know."

"Don't do that."

"Why not?"

"Because . . . don't."

"Okay, okay."

"I want to go home."

She was brushing her teeth when he came into the bathroom and started brushing too, standing right next to her. Which was unusual: over the years, without ever talking about it, they'd fallen into the habit of brushing separately.

He spat out: toothpaste, water, saliva. "When are you seeing him again?"

"Who?"

"Brad."

She spat. "I don't know."

The next day she was at the office when her phone buzzed: a Durham number she didn't recognize. But unknown numbers from all over were part of her job, so she thought little of it. Certainly she didn't expect it to be Ashley.

"Just checking in," she said. "I've been thinking about your questions. And what a sensitive situation you must be in."

Mel heard herself talking about the budget draft: the art and music classes it would save, the teacher raises it would set in stone, and of course the breakfasts it would put into the stomachs of hungry children. She talked about how hard she and Bradley had worked to make the idea palatable to Republicans and Democrats; she knew it was silly, she said, that something as simple as feeding children could possibly have a "conservative" and "liberal" side, but there it was.

"I get it," said Ashley. "I really do. Life is complicated." She wanted her to keep in mind that joining the group ("whatever we're going to call it") could take many forms, some more public than others. For example, if they did end up holding a protest march at the airport, maybe she and Art would decide not to actually march—but that didn't mean they couldn't help with planning. "There are options."

That night, over dinner she told Art what Ashley had said.

"You're really that worried about the budget?"

"I'm just telling you what Ashley told me."

"But I'm asking. Are you that worried about the budget?"

"I don't know. Maybe. And what about my work, too? What if no one wants to use me anymore because I'm known for—"

"Being against torture?"

"I'm just thinking out loud. Can you understand that? Can you understand that this is complicated and I'm just trying to think?"

He got up and took his dish to the sink. "Sure. I can understand that."

Later he joined her in the bathroom for teeth brushing again.

"I want to tell you what I'm thinking," he said. "Can I do that?"

"Of course."

"If this thing is happening, whatever it is, I want to be a part of it. I think it would feel strange not to be. I think it would feel bad. Does that make sense?"

"We used to do stuff like this all the time."

"But we stopped. We didn't even do the Iraq protests."

"There's more than one way to do good in the world," she said.

"It's true," he said, "we've helped people here."

"You mean your patients? Or your clients? Which is it now, patients or clients? I can never remember."

"Clients."

"So, that's what you're talking about? You helping your clients?" For the millionth time, the strangeness of it: all of his patients/clients, hundreds of them over the years, with whom he'd spent so many hours, and none of whom she had ever met. Thousands of hours of his life, invisible to her.

"But also the school board. This budget. Also helping people find where they're going to live. Treating them well, looking out for them."

"Now you're just buttering me up."

"I'm not."

"But I'll allow it."

One last burst of brushing for them both. He spat. She spat. Then he kissed her. "I love you, you know?"

"I know. I mean, I love you too. Sorry, that was bad. I love you."

The kiss became another. Became sex. Right there in the bathroom, standing up; the last time they'd done it that way had been years ago, when Michael was away at camp. Sex with Art was better than sex with Bradley. She'd never thought otherwise. Art was the person she wanted to have sex with for as long as she was still having sex, however long that was going to be.

So why?

Why why why why why?

"We'll decide together," he said afterward. "About the march, or the protest, or whatever it is. If it happens. We'll decide together, okay?"

"Okay."

"We're good?"

"We're good."

Later that night, unable to sleep, she sat at the dining room table with a pen and legal pad, trying to figure out what to say "in her own voice" to the people she was supposed to be writing to. Nothing came.

Before going back to bed, she checked her email. She had just one new message, from a person whose name she didn't recognize, a Carla Bratton:

Dear Mrs. Kinston,

You don't know me, but I read in the Herald *about the recent school board proposal for morning breakfasts and I want to say well done, I think it's wonderful. My own children are grown but my work means I have contact sometimes with young mothers across the county, and I know that many of them will find this program truly lightens their load. Not that they don't want to have breakfast ready each morning for their children, I know that many of them do, but for the days when it can't happen this program will be a relief. Thank you for fighting the good fight and getting it done, I will be sending similar notes and congratulations to your fellow board members. Good job!!!*

Thanks again,
Carla

When she was done, she saw a new message had arrived—from Michael. *Mom, did you get a chance to look into my question about our health insurance plan? Let me know when you do so I can cross it off my list.* She had no memory of him asking her anything about their health insurance. She almost even went to check with Art—maybe Michael had misremembered which parent he'd asked. But then she understood. Her son was using code, because he was afraid of what Art might see. *Health insurance* wasn't health insurance. *Health insurance* was Bradley. She had a brief vision of lifting the computer keyboard above her head and smashing it down on the table. *Working on it,* she wrote back. *Sorry for the delay!*

AYOUB

Habiba eats whatever food's put in front of her with equal relish, gains weight by the day, uses the litter box without prompting. She gets slightly less dusty looking. She leaps onto the windowsill and looks at the world like it's TV. She chases the balled-up rags he throws, pounces on them, bats them around with her paws. She chases pant legs, the hems of dresses, shoelaces, ice cubes dropped on the floor, specks of dust, insects. She prowls the apartment looking for mice she never finds, purrs when he pets her properly, and wiggles against him when not being petted properly, telling him to try something else.

She reminds him of a cat he used to know. Not a cat from his childhood. Not the lie he told Amira.

She reminds him of Yusuf.

No one knew how Yusuf got inside, though of course everyone had a theory. Some thought he'd snuck in through a ventilation shaft. But then why didn't he leave the same way? Was he lost? Confused? Was it possible he preferred the world of the prison to the world outside? The idea made them laugh, but what did they know? None of them had ever seen the prison's immediate surroundings. Perhaps there was nothing but inhospitable desert in every direction. Many of his fellow Moroccans assumed that they were in Tazmamart—and "everyone knew" Tazmamart was in the desert. One recurring theory held that Yusuf once belonged to a guard, but when this guard's wife delivered their first child, she banished the cat from their house, either because the baby was allergic or because the cat scratched its face. Every guard they ever asked rejected this theory, but the guards were liars, every word that came out of a guard's mouth was a lie, or at least the possibility had to be given serious consideration. Guards said they were in Tazmamart, were in Tagounite, were in Derb Moulay Cherif, were in a new prison with no name, which meant no one knew it existed, which meant no one talked about it, which meant they were forgotten. Not once, inside, did he hear the word *Temara*; he only knew for sure he was in Morocco from the guards' accents. No one knew how Yusuf got his name. A conspiratorial Pakistani man named Ali argued that the cat was a tool of the prison. If he wasn't seen for a few hours, most people assumed he was curled up resting in an air shaft somewhere. Ali, though, insisted he was in a back room with the guards, getting implanted with radio devices that made it possible for them to snoop on even their quietest conversations. Or getting injected with bacteria in hopes that he would spread disease among them. *Population control!* Ali shouted in Urdu, in English, in Arabic. *You know it's true!* No one put much stock in these theories. Everyone but Ali saved bits of food to lure Yusuf to their cells. Everyone agreed that once someone had successfully coaxed Yusuf into their company, no one else was to attempt coaxing him away for at least an hour. No one knew where this pact had originated, but everyone treated it as law, except none of them had watches, which meant all their fiercest arguments were about whether Yusuf had been with so-and-so for more than an hour or less than an hour. The guards made it worse: they lied about what time it was, contradicted each other, contradicted themselves. Same with prayer times. They brought rocks from outside and threw them at Yusuf, they kicked at Yusuf with their boots, they talked about grabbing Yusuf and stuffing him in a bag and adding bricks to the bag and throwing the bag in a lake. (Did that mean there was a lake nearby? Or was it just an expression? *Yes,* the guards said. *No,* the guards said. *If you wake up breathing water, the guards said, then you'll know about the lake.*) They talked about shooting Yusuf, running Yusuf over with a jeep, stepping on Yusuf's neck. But they never did any of it. *SEE?* Ali shouted, hoarse, down the hall. *THEY NEED HIM ALIVE TO FUCK WITH US, BROTHERS! THAT FUCKING CAT IS FUCKING WITH US!*

Habiba doesn't like it when he leaves. On the stairwell, he hears her paws scratching out their message—*no no no no no no no*—on the other side of the door. And then, usually, he stays.

He could bring her down with him—but what if she escaped?

She stops them from going to Avezzano. For the time being. Which he's genuinely sorry about. Eventually, he feels sure, they'll figure something out, whether it's taking her on the train or leaving her with someone. Like Bouchra, he suggests one day.

Never, says Amira. They will never leave the cat with Bouchra.

She notices what he notices. The roll of the mailman's cart on the street. The jangle of the mailman's keys as he lifts them to the mailbox lock. The second jangle as the mailbox door swings open. The click when it closes again. When he goes down for the mail, she doesn't paw at the door; she knows he'll be right back.

She likes prayer, which she seems to think is a game, a game where humans reach out in front of themselves for . . . what? She wants to know, she's curious, she wants to reach for it too, she darts around on the floor looking for it. Amira claims it annoys her, but he thinks he's seen it make her smile.

Habiba looks to him in the middle of the night when they're both woken by the cats fighting in the alley. Lets him put his hand on her head and wonder what she's thinking—wonder if, for her, the noises represent a nightmare from which she is grateful to have been rescued or, instead, her life, her real life, dangerous but free, the life she was meant for and to which, in her heart, she longs to return.

MEL

The second meeting of the North Carolina Anti-Torture Action Network has twice as many attendees as the first.

Despite several dozen emails on the group's new Listserv, no new name has emerged.

Again Linda leads them around:

Our oldest friends.

From way back.

The ones I was telling you about.

They live in Springwater.

Our oldest friends.

Murph has the list of agreed-upon tasks from last week, and he calls out for updates on each. People share news of website templates, server fees, Photoshop skills, sign-making supplies, applicable state laws on protest, county laws on protest, Springwater-specific laws on protest. Two gray-haired women who are either sisters or lovers who dress alike talk about having successfully made contact with a group in Ireland that has already held a protest at a small airport there linked to torture flights. The group wrote back a short note of support, which one of the women reads aloud, prefacing her reading with the disclaimer that she's obviously not going to attempt an Irish accent—and then doing exactly that.

"Ireland," Linda whispers in her ear. "Isn't that amazing?"

When it's "our Springwater people's turn" (Murph's words), Mel explains that they wrote their letters but have not yet received any replies. People ask if they have one of the letters to share, and she has to admit that she didn't think to bring a copy. She feels like she's back in school and hasn't done her homework. There's some talk of using Murph's laptop to pull up the email, but then no one can remember the Unitarians' Wi-Fi password. She's glad. The letters feel too personal to share, and at the same time not personal enough: generic, bloodless, too similar to what anyone would have written.

She leaves it to Art to give the update on their second job: identifying possible local supporters. She wonders if their list sounds as pathetic to everyone else as it does to her. Really, it's just guesses. Pastor Fred? Sheila from the school board? Sam, her old boss at Genova's? ("The sandwich place?" says Murph. "I love that place.") She has never thought of herself and Art as friendless people, but what their list—or lack of a list—has forced her to consider is the possibility that she's confused friendship and friendliness. Her coworkers, other basketball parents, other track-and-field parents, people she's helped find houses, their neighbors: there was plenty of friendliness there. But were any of them her actual friends?

Lying in bed two nights before, she wondered if it was this, as much as anything else, that explained Bradley. Maybe, without realizing it, what she'd wanted was a friend. Of course, she and Bradley weren't friends: friends talked about their lives openly, and if she and Bradley had talked openly, they would have admitted what they were up to—admitted it using the normal words, the clear words, *cheat* and *affair*— and that would have ruined it, and so they talked about school board business and had sex, and maybe the sex was just a placeholder for something else she hadn't known she was missing.

Had she and Art gone about life incorrectly? Shouldn't they have people in their lives they could talk to about anything at all, anytime? The way it used to be with Robert and Linda? She looks in her lap while Art speaks to avoid the expressions on everyone's faces, not wanting to see anything she might interpret as judgment.

"It sounds," says Linda, "like maybe at some point you'll need to just start putting the word out and see what happens. Going to people, but also giving people a chance to come to you."

"That could be," says Ashley. "But I think we also have to remember that we're not the ones living in Springwater. It might end up that the best thing for Mel and Art is to help us in a more behind-the-scenes way."

"Mmm," Mel says.

Murph suggests they move on to new business. Either he senses the awkwardness hanging in the air, or he's hell-bent on keeping them on schedule. Either way: new business. Either way: thank God for Murph.

Ashley goes first: it appears possible, she says, that the *Times* article will be running in two weeks, give or take. Of course, she says, that timeline isn't set in stone; she's been burned by the *Times* before. But she thinks they should start acting like it's happening—like the story's going to run in two weeks.

Art asks if this means the reporter has already talked to the on-paper owners.

Ashley says she doesn't know but assumes so.

"Can I make a proposal?" says Linda. She thinks they

should start planning an action at the airport for after the *Times* article runs, whenever that might be. A properly designed advance plan, she argues, will let them strike a balance between moving fast and maximizing participation. For example, they could agree that if the article is published on a Saturday, Sunday, Monday, Tuesday, or Wednesday, then the action will take place on the Saturday following publication. If it's published on a Thursday or Friday, it will happen on the *following* Saturday, giving more time for the word to spread and people to move plans. The exact details of the protest, says Linda, can be sorted out separately ("and we should probably set up a planning committee"), but one idea she has ("just for the sake of example") is for everyone to go to the airport, march to the Arcadian hangar, and attempt to deliver "citizens' indictments" to the company and its owners, plus a notice to the airport's owners that they are obligated—ethically but also legally—to evict Arcadian as a tenant, knowing the company is complicit in the violation of any number of laws, from the local to the international. This could all be accompanied, she says, by the delivery of dossiers on Arcadian's crimes to the offices of the governor, the district attorney, the county prosecutor, and the county sheriff. If they hear back in time from any Arcadian victims or their family members—she nods in Mel's direction—then they could include their stories, and maybe even their photographs, in the indictments, on their signs, in the dossiers. "I'm just thinking out loud," she says. "All this is for a committee to determine. But can we put the scheduling proposal to a vote right now?"

In the vote, Art gets a hand up right away. Everyone gets a hand up right away. Mel too. What else is she going to do?

Afterward people stand around talking, tidying up the basement, saying their hellos and goodbyes. Strangers keep finding their way to her and Art to ask them questions. About Springwater. About Bradley.

What's he like?

And you're on the PTA together?

The school board?

And what's that like?

A Republican, I heard?

Loves Dubya?

Old-boy type?

Country clubber?

Later, in the parking lot, Robert and Linda also ask mostly about Bradley. *Have you seen him? Talked to him? When will you? Of course, we know—we know we don't know exactly how he's involved—that's why we're asking, Melly, that's why we're asking.*

"God, it's exciting—isn't it?" says Art, drumming on the steering wheel. "Like the old days?"

"I guess."

"You're still worried about Brad?"

"I don't know."

"About the budget?"

"It's just . . . complicated."

"I know it's complicated."

They drive in silence for a while.

"You just put your hand up," she says.

"What?"

"We said we'd decide together."

"The scheduling vote? You voted for it too."

"But you did it first. Without me."

"It was just a scheduling vote. It wasn't saying we'd be there ourselves."

"So now you're saying you don't want to be there?"

"No, I'm saying that's not what this particular vote was about."

He takes a deep breath, then another; it's the kind of thing, she knows, that he teaches his patients to help them to avoid getting caught up in the rhythm of a moment, to slow down and give themselves room to identify what they actually think and feel and want.

"I'm sorry," he says. "You're right. I shouldn't have done it. I should have checked in with you."

She wishes that when it mattered, she'd known to slow down.

The next morning she has an appointment to show a townhouse on Clark Street to a young couple she knows only from the phone. She gets there fifteen minutes early to orient herself. She's inspecting the vent above the stove—trying to figure out where the smoke and steam actually go—when Michael calls.

"Well?" he says.

"What's up?" She hates her voice.

"Did you tell him?"

"I'm sorry, Michael, not yet. He's been working a lot."

"Okay."

"I'm sorry. I will." She wanders back to the foyer. Through the narrow vertical windows on either side of the front door—an architectural touch whose appeal she has never understood—she sees a red Kia being parked on the street. A man and a woman are in it, and she suspects they're the people she's meeting, until they get out and cross to the other side of the street.

When Michael speaks again, he sounds a decade younger. "Is it over?"

"Of course it's over. I told you it was over."

"Why'd you do it, Mom?"

"Oh, Michael. Would you believe me if I said I don't totally know myself?"

"Well, don't you think you should figure it out?"

The doorbell rings. "Hold on—hold on a second."

She opens the door and greets the young couple standing there with a series of hand gestures meant to communicate, *I'm finishing this call, sorry, show yourselves around, I'll be with you soon.*

"Are you showing a house right now?"

"Yes, but they're—"

"Jesus, Mom."

"Michael. Wait."

But he's gone.

The next morning they're woken early by a call from Linda. "Did you see it? Have you read it yet? I can't believe it's out already. Keith interviewed your school board guy and everything, or tried to. I have chills, Melly. I knew it was real, but this is something else. Keith did such a good job. Really, you have to read it. Read it and call me back."

It's a Monday, which means the protest is now set for Saturday.

Art brings a chair from the kitchen so they can sit together in front of the computer. They haven't had coffee yet, or even splashed water on their faces. Everything still has the softness of sleep. When was the last weekday morning that they did something together other than silently get ready for their respective workdays?

The story—"C.I.A. Expanding Terror Battle Under Guise of Charter Flights"—is right there on the *New York Times* home page, underneath an article about rising health insurance costs and above one about Kodak's plans to discontinue Kodachrome film.

Art clicks and up comes a photograph of an airplane on a runway at the Yew County Airport. It's bigger than the planes she usually sees there. Two men in jumpsuits appear to be inspecting the rear wheel. On the left side of the image, there's a blurry bit of brush, or a branch, creating the impression that the photographer hid behind a bush to avoid being seen while taking the picture.

The article has lots of information that is new to her and Art—and so, presumably, new to Linda and Robert and all the others. Arcadian is a descendant of Air America, an off-the-books airline operated by the CIA during Vietnam. After Congress shut it down, several of its core officers kept its mission alive by starting small charter flight companies in rural communities across the country. Over the years, Arcadian flights flew foreign leaders in and out of America for secret meetings, delivered guns and food to American-backed rebels in Africa and South America, and helped sneak American allies out of their home countries during times of unrest.

Bob Fox, the article says, was a famous Air America mechanic.

She wonders how many Arcadian employees are at this moment sitting at their computers, reading about themselves, about the company that signs their paychecks, knowing that people all around the country and the world are reading the same article. She wonders if they're picking up the phone and calling each other, trying to figure out what it means or might mean. Are they talking to their wives and girlfriends? Is it wrong to assume they're all straight men?

Apparently, Arcadian currently has seventy-nine employees, up from forty-three just a few years ago.

Apparently, Yew County was selected in part because the airport had no control tower, which meant less scrutiny.

She wonders if it's possible that, back in the Carlson Street era, when they heard—at a talk or a movie night or wherever—about torture in Latin America, they were, without realizing it, hearing about something where Arcadian was involved. She wishes she remembered more details from back then, but what she remembers most is her relief that she was finally learning the truth about the world.

One method used in setting up past C.I.A. proprietaries was to ask real people to volunteer to serve as officers or directors. Such an approach may have been used with Arcadian Airlines. William J. Rogers, 84, of Maine, said he was asked to serve on the Arcadian board in the 1980s because he was a former Navy pilot and past national commander of the American Legion. He knew the company did government work, but not much more, he said. "We used to meet once or twice a year," he said.

Arcadian's president, according to corporate records, is Bradley Welk, a Springwater-based lawyer who is an officer or a member of several local charities and community organizations, including the school board.

Asked about his role with Arcadian, Mr. Welk said only: "Most of the work we do is for the government. It's on the basis that we can't say anything about it."

Asked whether he was aware that Arcadian flights appeared to be implicated in extraordinary rendition operations, Mr. Welk declined to comment.

"Jesus," says Art.

"Do you think he knew?"

"I don't know. Probably. I don't know. What do you think? You know him better."

"I don't know. Now I feel like I don't know him at all."

Linda calls again, asking if they've read the article yet, asking what they think, asking if they've heard yet from "any other Springwater people," asking how they feel about marching now that the march is officially happening. She knows they had their reservations, but what do they think now? "Have you heard from any of the survivors you wrote to yet? Or the survivors' wives? Have they seen this? Maybe you should write to them again now that the article is out. You could send them the article."

"Maybe."

"Is there anyone local you should be sending the article to? Like the pastor guy, people like that?"

"Pastor Fred, maybe, yeah."

"I mean, it's the *Times*—people will take that seriously."

She decides to exempt herself from the task of trying to explain to Linda that the *Times* is not as universally respected as she seems to think. She decides not to bring up how, just a few years ago, in more than one "IRAQ ACTION BLAST," Linda herself identified the *Times* as a fundamentally untrustworthy news source, guilty of uncritically regurgitating lies on behalf of the CIA.

"And what about your guy, Welk?"

"What about him?"

"Have you heard from him?"

"Why would I have heard from him?"

"I don't know, Melly. School board stuff? I'm just asking."

"Well, I haven't."

"It must be so creepy," Linda says. "To know someone like that. I literally have goosebumps. I'm sitting here looking at goosebumps forming on my arms just from thinking about it."

A showing, the bank, another showing, the post office: wherever she is, she listens as hard as she can listen and doesn't hear a single person talking about the *Times* article, Arcadian, the CIA, torture. Which of course doesn't mean that none of them have read it. After all, she's read it, and she's not saying anything. Everyone she sees, everyone she passes, the people she shows houses to, the people whose houses she shows: each of them could know, could have read the article, could have no idea, could be one of the seventy-nine Arcadian employees tallied by the *Times*.

It's true, she decides: she doesn't really have friends in Springwater. If she had friends, she would call one of them now to talk about the article. Heading into Genova's for a late lunch, she hopes that Sam is there and it will turn out he read it, so they can talk about it.

Maybe Sam is her Springwater friend.

But Sam's not there. The girl behind the cash register asks if Mel wants to leave a message, and she says thanks but no, that's okay, she'll catch him later. Next time. Nothing urgent.

She calls Art in the car. "I need to tell you something."

"Okay." He sounds so resigned that again she's sure he already knows. Maybe Michael, in his frustration at her delay—at what she, his mom, has forced him to bear—called and told him. Maybe Michael didn't tell him but he knows anyway. Maybe he almost knows. Knows without fully knowing. She has always felt that, were Art ever to cheat, she would automatically know right away.

"I want to be there, at the airport. If you still do."

"Really?"

"Really."

"What changed your mind? The article?"

"I guess so."

"Okay, so—great. We're doing it."

"It's just that, before we do . . ."

"Yeah?"

"It might sound crazy."

"Go ahead, sound crazy."

"I want to talk to Bradley. Face-to-face. I want to hear what he says."

"That's respectable," he says. "I respect that. Just don't get your hopes up."

"Consider my hopes down."

"And probably meet somewhere public, right? Just to be safe. Who knows what he'll do if he's pissed off?"

"Yeah." She senses an opening, and senses herself rushing toward it. "I think his marriage is on the rocks, too." She has no idea if it is or isn't, but saying so now might help her later.

"Really?"

"I'm not sure, but maybe."

"Bad time for Brad, then. Just meet in public, okay?"

"I will," she says. "That's a good idea."

BRADLEY

When he gets to Genova's, she's sitting at a booth in the back with a Diet Coke. It's obvious she's still angry. But why? Because she didn't think the Benson prank was funny? He apologized for that. Because they got caught? That wasn't his fault any more than it was hers. He shouldn't have come; her anger is unfair, and unfairness isn't what he needs today. She tells him she hasn't ordered any food and isn't going to, she's not hungry. Who invites someone to a restaurant at dinnertime, then says they won't eat? Pure manipulation. He shouldn't have come.

"I saw you in the *Times* today."

He groans, a louder groan than he would have picked had it been at all voluntary.

What was he thinking, taking a call from the *New York Times*? He should have hung up. No comment. First because that was the playbook. Second because even if it wasn't the playbook, talking to the *New York Times* was a losing proposition. He had nothing to hide and nothing to be ashamed of, but he should have known that the story would be subtly constructed to communicate the exact opposite. That even if they quoted him accurately, his words would be deployed to support whatever the writer had already decided to write, the vision of reality his paper sold day by day to its readers, who mistook that vision for the truth.

Asked whether he was aware that Arcadian flights appeared to be implicated in extraordinary rendition operations, Mr. Welk declined to comment.

Well, yes. At that point in the interview, he *declined to comment.* He hung up. Said nothing. Freedom of speech, he feels quite sure, also covers freedom of nonspeech. Freedom not to say anything. Freedom of silence. But in the *Times* story there's no such thing, and his silence is pressed into service, forced to become part of the story that *Times* readers already know they want: a story in which the president of a company with any link of any kind to *extraordinary rendition* is obviously guilty and obviously knows it.

Extraordinary rendition! Why couldn't they use simple terms? Why couldn't they say *the transportation of prisoners*?

It's all horseshit. It's an industrial vat filled past the brim and overflowing with hot liquefied horseshit.

"Well, I'm ordering," he says. "It's dinnertime, and we're at a restaurant, so—I'm ordering." At the counter he asks for a turkey-and-bacon sandwich and salt-and-vinegar chips. He shouldn't have answered a call from a New York number. He should have hung up before the reporter got started. He shouldn't be in Genova's with Melanie. He should leave with his chips, turn and leave and be gone and lose nothing but a turkey-and-bacon sandwich.

"That story was bullshit," he says, sliding back in the booth.

"Which part, exactly?"

"The whole thing."

"It's not true?"

"I'm not talking about this or that part being true."

"So what are you talking about?"

"I'm saying the whole thing is extremely naive."

"I want to ask you a question," she says. "And I want you to tell me the truth. Can you do that?"

"Maybe."

"You can't say you'll tell me the truth?"

"It's not that," he says. Sam arrives with his sandwich, seems to intuit that they're in the middle of something, and ducks out. He's always liked Sam. "Everyone has things they can't necessarily just talk about whenever they want. That's not lying. That's not evil. That's just reality."

"Did you know?"

"Know what?"

"Did you know what you were signing up for?"

"Why do you care so much?"

"It's illegal. It's pain and suffering, and it's illegal, and it's wrong."

"What is?"

"Torture."

"Ah."

"What?" she says.

"People call a lot of different things torture."

"Bradley."

"I just think, Melanie, that we probably see things very, very differently. On this subject, at least. And I think, at the end of the day, that's probably all there is to say about it." He bites into his sandwich. Chews. "Let's talk about something else. Let's talk about our situation with your son. Is it under control?"

She looks at him with pure hatred, and he marvels at the mystery of how he was ever attracted to the tired-looking, judgmental woman across the table. The first time they fucked, she moved underneath him in total understanding.

Looking at her now, he doesn't quite believe it's the same person. She's still glaring—because, she claims, she cares about what's *illegal*, cares about what's *wrong*, cares about *pain and suffering*. But if that's what she really cares about, aren't there better places to start than Arcadian Airlines of Springwater, North Carolina?

"It's under control," she says.

"He's not going to make trouble for us?"

She shakes her head.

"Is that a no? As in, no, he's not going to make trouble?"

"That's a no."

He still has half his sandwich left, and he's determined to finish it; he paid for it, after all. If she doesn't like sitting with him, she can move. If she wants to sit there glaring at him, he can take it. She's the one who invited him. He sits and chews and waits to see who's going to break first, who's going to get up and leave, and he knows it won't be him.

In his truck, he calls Sheri and tells her he has to take care of a few things at the office before he can come home.

"Good meeting with Mel?" she says.

"Yeah, good." She thinks they were discussing school board business.

She says nothing about the article, which he assumes means she hasn't read it. He imagines—moving his lips but rarely forming real words—trying to explain. Explain to Melanie, explain to Sheri, explain to whomever. It must be similar to being a soldier, he thinks. Not the same—he's not crazy— but similar. Your country calls. You answer, and seeing the answer through lets you glimpse the normally invisible gears turning beneath the surface of the world. Reality. History.

Anyone can read about the gears in the paper or hear about them on the news. Anyone can see photographs that appear to reveal the truth of the gears' inner workings. But none of that tells you anything. When you watch the news, you don't see the gears, even when you think you do. Maybe especially when you think you do. You don't know what it means to answer the call. Only soldiers know.

Where would a country be without people answering the call?

Which isn't to say no mistakes are ever made. Nothing's perfect. But unless you know—unless you've actually caught a glimpse of the gears—you're not qualified to judge.

He sends all the windows down, letting in as much wind and dark as possible. No radio, no CD. Night sounds, wind sounds. He thinks of his dad, how it felt to be in the car with him at night, inside the little metal world gliding through the universe. He remembers the sunroof and presses the button that activates the mechanism that slides it open, and more wind comes in, and the wind moves differently. He improvises a long way home, adding ten minutes to what could have been a fifteen-minute trip, and when he gets to his house, he doesn't turn at the driveway, he keeps driving, telling himself the moment's so beautiful it would be a shame to let it end.

AYOUB

He's awake in the dark on the floor. Habiba's watching him, curious to see whether he's really up or going back to sleep. He stays on the floor and lets the cat press against his chest, telling him whatever she's trying to tell him.

He hears Amira get up and shower, hears the spoon scooping coffee beans, the spoon clinking against the coffeepot, the stovetop clicking, the flame rushing up. It's not too late to push up from the floor, go out into the apartment, ask his wife how he can help this morning, and what he can do to be helpful while she's gone at work.

That's what he did yesterday.

That's what he did the day before that.

He could do it today.

He could do it now.

But then he hears the front door open, and then he hears it close, and then it's just him and Habiba.

He showers. He dresses. He leaves the apartment, walking toward the market, tilting his head down just enough to avoid eye contact with people he passes but not so much that he's ever in danger of running into anything. He lifts his feet properly: no shuffling, no tripping. He wonders if this obsessive focus on his own presentation in the world is the kind of thing that makes flat men flat—if it starts with them creating a protective layer between themselves and the world, which then hardens in place, turning a shield into a cage.

Sometimes, walking down the street, he feels sure that he's about to run into Arsalan, that Arsalan's coming around the corner, that Arsalan's about to step out of a store and be there, right in front of him.

At the market he heads to Walid's produce stall, which means passing by the butcher stall; he keeps his eyes down, not wanting to see or be seen by any of his former coworkers. He pretends to be inspecting the fruit, attempting to make the facial expressions of a man who isn't sure what he's looking for and, in fact, doesn't know if he'll buy anything at all. A man who hasn't already reclassified the "fruit money" portion of his weekly allowance as "helping with Habiba money." A man shopping casually, just for the pleasure of being in the market. He looks out of the corner of his eye for Walid, listens for the low murmur of his voice. The market moves around him.

"Can I help you?" says the young man behind the cashbox. One of Walid's nephews.

"Is Walid here?"

The nephew makes a twitchy motion that says he doesn't care enough to shrug, then looks down at his phone. "How should I know?"

Either the nephew knows who Ayoub is and has decided that who he is makes him deserve being blown off with a not-even shrug, or he doesn't know who Ayoub is and has decided to treat him this way simply because of how pathetic he looks: stooped and thinned and powerless and not the kind of person who gets to ask where Walid is.

Already, in his mind, he's walking home. Walking into the

foyer. Checking the mailbox even though he knows the mail never comes this early. Working his way up the stairs. Lying on the floor. Waiting for Habiba.

Just when he's about to give up, there's a rustling behind the nephew and it's Walid, coming through the curtain of plastic flaps that separates the customer-facing part of the stall from the employees-only back area. He's moving slowly, struggling with a box loaded to the top with melons. Ayoub sees him first—sees, too, that the nephew is still looking at his phone—and hurries over as quickly as he can to help Walid carry the box to a table. Once upon a time, he could have reached his arms under the box and taken the whole thing himself and told Walid to point wherever it belonged. Now just taking half—or maybe less—of its weight pushes everything out of his mind besides a single unpleasant truth: he is nothing but pieces of flesh and bone, stitched together by nothing but flesh and bone.

"Thanks for that," Walid says, in Arabic, once they've set the box down.

The nephew is looking up from his phone now, glaring like he would hate him if he could be bothered to spend the energy.

"What brings you my way?" says Walid, in Arabic. "Need another crate?"

"No," he says, in Italian. "It's not that."

Walid switches to Italian too. "What, then?"

He is very much aware that it's his turn to talk. The nephew's glare takes on a more gleeful tint, like he's celebrating Ayoub's inability to communicate. There's nothing left to do but prove him wrong—nothing to do but look Walid in the eye and make with the muscles of his throat and mouth and tongue the combination of movements that adds up to asking if he could possibly have a job, any job, he'll do anything, really.

Walid nods, then nods again, and then he nods again. They're not *Yes, of course* nods, they're *I'm thinking* nods. He points his chin in the direction of the butcher's stall. "Ahmed won't have you back?"

"They hired someone else."

In fact, two weeks after he got back, Ahmed stopped Amira on the street and told her that Ayoub should feel free to stop by—that his old job was his, if he wanted it. He went over the next day, and from the moment he stepped behind the counter, he knew it was impossible: the metallic smell of the meat, the bones, the knives, the blood draining on the floor in the back. Just standing there made his wrists ache like he'd already been cutting for hours. Ahmed must have seen it on his face. "Maybe another time," he said, using a voice Ayoub had never heard him use. The voice he likely used for talking to his children. "There's no rush."

He has to hope Walid's question isn't a test—that he hasn't talked to Ahmed and heard what happened. "They hired someone else," he says again, "and now they can't just let that person go. Plus, I'm tired of working with meat. I'll do anything. Really, I will."

"You know," says Walid. "Your wife . . . I've been very impressed with her. It can't have been easy."

"No."

"She must be a strong person."

"Yes. Of course, yes."

"A good wife."

"Yes."

"You're trying to do your part. Give her some relief."

"Exactly, yes, that's exactly what I'm trying to do. Also, we just adopted a cat." From the shape of Walid's frown, he knows he should switch gears. "It's like you said. I need to do my part."

Walid puts his hands on his stomach and gazes off across the market. Without moving his eyes at all, he orders his nephew to go tidy up the back room. On his way past them, he mutters something Ayoub can't make out.

"To be honest," says Walid, "I could use some help." What he needs, he explains, is for someone to be on hand part time, during the stretches that are typically the stall's busiest, to do whatever it takes to keep things moving as quickly as possible, whether it's moving produce from the shelves underneath the tables up to the tabletops as needed, going to the back for refills as needed, sweeping as needed. As he describes the job, he looks Ayoub up and down. "It's probably not what you're looking for," he says. "It's a lot of lifting. Just . . . lifting, lifting, lifting."

That's fine, he almost blurts out, *that's perfect.* But he swallows the words and makes a face that he hopes is the face of someone mulling an offer's pros and cons. "I think that could work," he says. "In fact, I'm really only looking for part-time now."

"Well, okay. Let's try it." Walid tells him how much he can pay and proposes a one-week trial period, starting tomorrow. "Just to make sure you actually like it."

He remembers to add that he can work any day besides Sundays and Tuesdays, because these are Amira's days off, and after so many days apart he doesn't want any more.

Walid says he can have Sundays and Tuesdays off, as long as he doesn't tell the other employees—the nephews—that he asked for it. "It's better if it sounds like my idea," he says.

He also asks him not to share how much he's paid. "It's only right that I pay you more, because you're older and you have a wife. But they won't understand. They'll get jealous."

He agrees. It's been a long time since another person has asked him to keep a secret, and he feels a nourishing warmth as the information he's been asked not to repeat nestles inside him.

He asks Walid not to tell anyone yet. "I want to be sure to give Amira the news myself. Even if it's just a one-week trial."

"Of course. Absolutely, yes. That's sweet, Ayoub. I like it."

The rush of victory carries him most of the way home, and it's only when he's about to step into the foyer that he begins to reckon with the fact that, starting tomorrow, he is actually going to work at the produce stall, lifting box after box, setting them down, assuming responsibility for not dropping anything. Walking up the stairs, he can't stop his brain from projecting a slideshow of horrible images: Habiba dead on the living room floor, Habiba dead on the spare room floor, Habiba dead on the kitchen floor, Habiba nowhere to be found, the apartment empty. But no: she's still there. Not dead. Of course she's not. She's alive. They lie on the floor and playfully swipe at each other and he laughs out loud with relief and for the five minutes that follow he's more content than he's been in a long time.

Her fur's not the same color as Yusuf's, she's not the same size as Yusuf, she has few of Yusuf's mannerisms. But she has the same hazel-green eyes as Yusuf, and they move in their sockets with the same slow serenity.

He gets up and starts cleaning: vacuums, mops, wipes the countertops, the stovetop, the cabinets. He needs to build his stamina, and he needs to do more for Amira, and here he is, doing both at once.

He knows what he did was wrong. It's wrong for a husband to bring an animal into the house without asking his wife, and wrong to insist that the animal stay when it's obvious that she hates the idea. And understanding this has no impact on the ferocity of his desire that Habiba stay. Anything else—impossible. But he can do more. He has to do more. He has to do his part.

Habiba hides in the spare room until he's done vacuuming, and she's just settled onto the couch when her head jerks up, her eyes fixed on the door. Then he hears it too: the jangle of the mailman's keys as he lifts them to the lock. Early today. The second jangle as the mailbox door swings open. The click as the door closes.

On the stairs, he wills his breathing to stay steady, his pulse to stay steady; he tells himself it doesn't matter, he's here, he's free, he's home.

Can his memory be trusted? There are sentences he remembers writing but can't find in the shoebox, no matter how many times he looks. So maybe he never wrote them. Maybe he wrote them and threw them away. Maybe he wrote them and they never got sent. The guards told them as much—*We just toss 'em*—but the guards were liars. The same guards came around handing out paper and pens, saying write now, because who knew when they would be allowed to write again. The pens were always at the end of their lives, barely any ink, you sometimes had to try several times to form a single letter, you ripped the cheap paper. Ali refused to write any letters at all, insisting that the whole exercise was an elaborate punishment, one he refused to consent to. *All of the effort of communication,* he said, *and none of the reward. They want us talking and talking and thinking no one cares.* Ali was crazy, which didn't mean Ali was wrong. But then the guards would come around again with cheap paper and mostly dead pens and he wouldn't be able to resist.

Maybe he wrote those sentences. Maybe in letters that got sent. Maybe Amira read them, and when he asked if there were any more letters, she lied. Maybe she kept them somewhere separate. A different shoebox. Maybe she destroyed them. Maybe she destroyed them and doesn't even remember destroying them, has succeeded in wiping every particle of their existence from her mind, which is exactly what he wants to do, but he can imagine only one way of doing it, which is for the letters to prove they existed by arriving, by coming to him so he can destroy them. Burn them. Or shred them into small pieces and put the small pieces in a glass of water and let the water disintegrate them and send the slurry of disintegrated pieces down the sink.

But today, when he opens the mailbox, there's no Red Cross envelope. Today there's only bills.

When Amira gets home, she shows no signs of noticing his cleaning. Or she notices but feels the need to pretend she doesn't, as if doing so would mean surrendering her right to be angry about Habiba. She asks what he wants for dinner, and he says—because he means it—that she should make whatever she feels like. She insists that he pick: she doesn't want to go to the trouble of making something he doesn't actually want. He says he'll eat anything. Fine, she says, if that's the case, she's just going to heat up some roasted vegetables and noodles.

All night he keeps falling asleep only to jerk awake, sure that he's late for his first shift, or that he's missed it altogether. Each time, Habiba jerks up too, looking into his eyes to ask him what's wrong.

At dawn he prays into the new day, into the dark becoming light, into the stream of life, pleading to be let in.

Right after Amira leaves for work, he realizes that he should have told her about the produce stall, not just because she deserves to know what he's doing but also because she could have given him words of support he could have carried with him, making him that much less likely to turn and run and pretend it never happened. But it's too late, she's gone, and by the time he thinks to call her cell phone, it's too late for that too: her shift has started. Texting doesn't feel right.

He messages Mourad instead: *hey bud.*

Mourad responds right away: *heyyyyyyyy!!*

what's up

To which he responds: *starting new job today*

selling veggies

haha

To which Mourad, who keeps track of equipment repairs and purchases for a small construction company, responds:

dude, yes!!!!

awesome

good job

These same words, coming from anyone else in his life, would feel unbearably condescending. But from Mourad they unlock some previously hidden source of strength inside him. Maybe it's just because they've known each other so long, but sometimes he wonders if it has anything to do with the fact that one of Mourad's uncles, one he met many times, was known to have spent time in Tazmamart. He can't remember how he knew this, but he remembers going with Mourad to sit with this uncle and drink tea, remembers how the uncle said almost nothing and he and Mourad talked and talked about anything—school, sports, girls—their words pulled out of them faster and faster by an unspoken sense that if they were to stop, they would find themselves in a silence that none of them wanted to hear. He doesn't know if this uncle is still alive; Mourad hasn't mentioned him, just like he hasn't said anything about Temara. He assumes at some point Amira told him something.

He feels ready. Ready for his first-ever shift as a part-time trial employee of Walid's produce stall. Walking to the market, he keeps his head up, not seeking eye contact but not avoiding it either, letting people see that he is one of them, with somewhere to go and something to do when he gets there.

For the two and a half hours that constitute his first shift, his life consists of one thing only: attention on the task before him. Which tabletop spots are getting empty, which under-table shelves are getting empty, what Walid needs from him next, and next after that, and next after that. What he's supposed to be lifting, where he's supposed to be setting it down, the urgency of not spilling anything or knocking anything over. The mean nephew from yesterday isn't there; it's a different nephew today. If, God forbid, he drops something and it gets bruised or broken or stepped on, does the cost come out of his pay? He doesn't know. What is Walid thinking about his performance? He doesn't know. He needs to pay attention to the task before him. Sweat beads on his forehead and runs salty into his eyes. His muscles tell him that they can't take it anymore, and he tells them they're wrong. People are seeing him. People may be talking about him. Word may have reached the butcher stall: *Guess who's . . . Did you hear . . .*

Oh well.

His body sings pain and soon the intensity bears no relation to what he's doing or not doing that second, it's constant. He doesn't stop. He doesn't drop anything. He doesn't ask for a break. And then his shift's over.

"Well done," says Walid. "You did well." He takes a wad of bills from his pocket and starts peeling off his payment for the day. "I imagine it's a bit boring for you, though. A bit basic, maybe?"

It takes him a moment to understand that he's being offered an out: a chance to quit without admitting that the job is too physically tough. "Not too basic for me." He realizes that he's smiling. A real, unforced smile. "I had fun."

"Well, okay. I mean, good. But remember not to tell the others how much I pay you. They won't like it."

He mimes zipping his lips shut, and for whatever reason that makes Walid laugh. It's the first time he's seen Walid laugh, and the first time in years that anyone has really laughed in response to something he's done, and now he's smiling so hard he worries that he might be blushing, or worse, about to weep.

At home Habiba eyes him warily. Maybe he smells different, thanks to all the sweat. It's good to have a shower that's for something other than basic upkeep—a shower that's immediately necessary for the removal of stench and sweat earned through hard work. Since his return, the bathroom mirror has functioned mostly as something to be avoided. But after his shower he looks at his reflection and it's different. He knows this is mostly, or even entirely, a trick played on his mind by the brain chemicals that come with effort and persistence and victory. He doesn't care. He moves to see the stranger in the glass from different angles, flirting with the notion that it's actually him.

Once he's dressed, he writes Mourad again: *first shift down. made it. haha.*

Mourad responds: *dude yessssss!*

The wheels of the mailman's cart rolling on the street; he and Habiba lock eyes, each asking the other if they heard it too.

The jangle of the mailman's keys as he lifts them to the lock.

The second jangle.

The closing click.

On the way down the stairs, he tells himself that if there are more letters coming, then today is a good day for it. This feels true enough that he experiments with telling himself that he doesn't care anymore whether they're coming or not, whether they exist or not, whether Amira read them or not.

No Red Cross envelope today. Just something from Amira's mother. He leaves it in the mailbox so she won't think he's obsessed with the mail.

Back upstairs, his victory at the produce stall keeps running through him, washing him clean.

When they first moved into the apartment, the day after they were married, there was a stretch of days—three, maybe, though it felt like longer—during which neither of them was ever alone there. It wasn't something planned; it just happened. If they left, they left together, and came back together, too—until one day they went for a walk together and parted ways at the market, where Amira stayed to buy food while he continued down the street to the hardware store to buy shelves for the closet. He got back to the apartment first and only then realized that he'd never been alone there before. It only lasted about half an hour, but for that half hour he felt something new he couldn't name: a new variety of loneliness and a new variety of relief rolled into one. When he heard Amira coming up the stairs, he was so happy that he ran to the door, yanked it open, stood on the landing, and called down: "Hello, you!" The new feelings ran through him like wind celebrating itself by running through trees in summer, begging the leaves and branches to move along with it. It became a routine, every few weeks: "Hello, you!"

Now, hearing Amira on the steps, he jumps up from the sofa and goes to stand on the landing, remembering at the last minute to pull the door shut behind him so Habiba can't escape. "Hello, you!"

If he's seen a more obligatory smile in his life, he can't remember.

"Remember?" he says when she's made it up to the landing. "Remember I used to say that?"

"I remember."

As soon as they're inside the apartment, Habiba lunges, play-attacking the hem of Amira's dress as a way of welcoming her home. But Amira doesn't know it's a game, or knows but refuses to admit it. "Get off!" She kicks in the cat's direction. "Go away! Damn it!" Habiba keeps lunging; she still thinks they're playing.

He steps between them and shoos the cat away.

"I can't come home and be attacked by an animal."

"She was just playing."

"That wasn't playing."

"We'll figure it out. She'll learn."

"Oh, you know the future?"

"I promise," he says. "You'll see. Guess what I did today?"

"I have no idea. What?"

He reaches into his pocket and pulls out his day's pay.

"What's that?" She looks alarmed, like she's afraid that he stole the money and that by taking the bills from his hand, or even just by looking at them, she will become complicit in the theft.

"From Walid."

"He just gave it to you?"

"No, no." He explains about the job.

She asks why she's just learning this now.

"I know I should have told you. But I wanted it to be a surprise."

Finally she takes the bills. Counts them. "All this for just a few hours?"

In her voice he hears the suggestion that Walid paid him the amount that he did not as compensation for his age or the fact that he's married but as an expression of pity. Of course, the thought has crossed his mind. But so what? It's the same money either way. He did the job as well as it was possible to do it. "I thought you'd be happy," he says. "I thought it would help."

"Of course it will. Of course. I'm just tired."

That night, lying on the floor of the spare room, he is happy to realize that he's about to sleep through the night, and this happiness is marred only slightly by the thought that he should be getting up and joining Amira in her room. Their room. In their bed. But it's too late. In Temara he was always asleep and never asleep, he could sleep for ten, eleven, twelve hours at a time, only it wasn't sleep, it was something else. And it's often like that still, here in the apartment, but in a way worse, because he's supposed to be home again. It's supposed to be over. And tonight it is. For now. He's actually falling asleep. He's actually sleeping.

The next day he shows up at the produce stall ten minutes early. "Tell me what to do," he says to Walid. All he can do is hear Walid's instructions and pass them on to his body and see what happens. It's busier today than yesterday—more lifting, more to set down, more to keep track of—but now he's done it before. His muscles beg. *We're still healing,* they say. *Please.* There's nothing to do but keep going, do whatever's next, whatever Walid asks, take note of what he feels but not allow those feelings to mean anything, not let them stop him or slow him down or make him drop a box. Every second he finds out whether he's made it through, and every next second he decides to find out whether he can make it through again, and then he decides to find out again, and then he decides to find out again, and then again, and then again.

MEL

"Let me see if I'm understanding what you're trying to tell me." Pastor Fred leans forward and sets his elbows on his desk, then his forearms, resting them on top of a printed-out copy of the *Times* article like he's preparing to use them as implements for sorting true from false, important from irrelevant. "Okay?"

It seems that he's actually waiting for an answer.

"Okay," says Mel.

They're in his office, in the basement of the United Methodist Church of Springwater, which is a lot like the basement of the Raleigh Unitarian Church, but with more carpeting and less sunlight.

They have to start somewhere.

So here they are.

"As I understand it, from what you've told me and what this article seems to say, Arcadian Airlines is a business."

"Well, a pretend business," says Art. "They're not actually 'in business.' They're not trying to make a profit or find customers or anything else a real business does." They've already explained this, but if Art is frustrated at having to say it again, he doesn't show it. She makes a note to compliment him for his patience later.

"Okay, but—stick with me. If Arcadian Airlines is a business—or, like you said, a business-like entity—then my first question is: What service is that business providing? And from what I can tell, the answer is simple: they provide transport. Flights. A to B, B to C. Do I have that right?"

"Yes," says Art. "But—"

"I know. I know there's more to it than that. Just stick with me for a second. You two have concerns about what happens on the other end of these flights. And I find that so admirable, I really do. But at the same time, it seems important not to lump together things that are actually separate. Arcadian Airlines provides a service. That service is transit. And what I'm wondering is whether it's fair to put so much scrutiny on a company that's just providing transit."

Someone knocks quietly on the door; somehow Pastor Fred knows who it is, because he calls out to the person by name—Lois—telling her he's busy, but he'll be sure to find her when he's done. "Think about it this way. Say we have an ax murderer. Or a gang of ax murderers. Okay? Just an example. A thought exercise." She doesn't really know anything about Pastor Fred—just that Bradley had reason to think he'd support the breakfast subsidy, and that Bradley turned out to be right. She's only ever heard him talk about breakfast, and she loved what he had to say: how breakfast—food, eating, basic sustenance—couldn't be an issue with a Democratic side and a Republican side, with liberal and conservative positions. Children needed to be fed, and that was that. If his congregants didn't like hearing him say so, that wasn't for him to worry about. That was between them and God. "So you find out about these ax murderers. And you're upset. You don't like the sound of it. And then—just hold on one more second, Art, I'm getting there, I promise—you find out all the ax murderers in this gang of ax murderers get around using this one particular bus line. Or whatever it is. One particular cab company they always call. Are you following me? What I'm trying to say is, I'm not sure I can see that it would make sense, at that point, to really go after the bus line. As opposed to going after the ax murderers. I mean, the people at the bus company—they're just doing their jobs." He frowns. "Now, it's not that I'm trying to say that these practices—these interrogation practices, these alleged interrogation practices—are in any way the equivalent of ax murder. This is just a thought exercise."

Mel experiences the words coming from his mouth as a steady flow of liquid concrete that, without some interference, will at any moment begin to harden around her, fixing her to the carpeted floor forever.

"I hear what you're saying," says Art. "But I'm not sure the analogy works for me."

"No?"

"I think it would be more accurate to say that what we have here is a gang of ax murderers that started their own taxi company for the specific purpose of hiding their murders."

"But none of the bus drivers are murdering anyone. They're just flying buses. Excuse me, driving buses."

"That's not the point, though."

"You have a problem, but you're not actually focusing on the problem. You're focusing on a transportation company."

"So you won't help us, then," says Mel. Art gives her a sharp look, like he thinks she's surrendering too soon. But if that's what he thinks, he's wrong. Being here is pointless.

"I just don't think I can see it," says Pastor Fred. "And I'm aware that saying that might testify as much to my own limitations as anything else. I would never claim to be without limitation. But no, I can't see it." He looks sad, like he really does wish he could see it. "And when did you say it was? Your protest?"

"We didn't," says Art.

"Ah."

"Can I ask one more question before we go?" says Art.

"Of course. I'm in no rush. It doesn't have to be just one."

"Put Arcadian aside for a minute. What about just torture? Guantánamo? Abu Ghraib? Can you tell us, right here—no more analogies—what you think? As a man of God? As a person? I mean, have you seen the photographs?"

"I do remember some pictures that made the news. And I understood they were leaked out illegally, which of course I can't condone."

"But torture. Are you against it?"

"I'd rather comment on a specific scenario. Not something so general."

"So you're not against torture in general?"

"In my line of work, what I've learned is, it's really best to stay focused on the specifics."

"Well, okay. You're not against torture. Good to know."

"I didn't say that, Art. I said—"

"We heard you," says Art. "I don't think there's anything left to talk about."

Anyone watching Pastor Fred lead them upstairs would have no idea what they had been talking about; his face betrays nothing but pastoral calm. When they're out the door, he calls Mel's name. "This is completely unrelated, but . . . what happened with the budget?"

And this is how Mel and Art learn that the Republican members of the school board have drawn up a new draft budget, one they plan to introduce at the next public meeting. Pastor Fred doesn't specify who told him, and claims not to know exactly how this new draft differs from the old one. The only thing he knows for sure is: no more breakfasts. "You really haven't heard about this?"

"Okay," says Art in the car. "I guess Bradley got pissed."

The next meeting is with Sheila Pacon, at her house. They decide Art should wait in the car.

She has no choice but to tell Sheila what she's just heard from Pastor Fred. There's no more room in her, she wants to think, for any kind of lie, even a plausibly deniable lie of omission.

"What are you saying, Mel? Why would they do this?"

"I don't know. I just heard from Pastor Fred a few minutes ago."

"Can't you ask Bradley? I mean, aren't you two sort of close?"

"I wouldn't say *close.*"

"But this was your thing, the compromise."

"I don't know," she says. "I'm in the dark."

"Is it related to all this?" She holds up the *Times* article. Not a computer printout, the real thing. "This CIA stuff?"

"I don't know," she says. "Maybe."

"But how?"

"I don't know."

"Was he playing us? Some kind of mind games thing? Does he know about this group you've joined?"

"I don't know."

"Jesus. Okay." Sheila's cat skitters into the room and launches itself into her lap. "Of course it's horrible," she says, gesturing at the *Times* article. "Those photographs? I didn't sleep for weeks. But I have to ask you, Mel. I don't know what's going on here, but is there any chance that you call off this march thing and Bradley comes back to the table?"

She tells Sheila the march isn't her "thing" to call off; it's a group effort with a life of its own. She's just the messenger.

Sheila, she can tell, is only half listening—is thinking about how she can get her hands on a copy of the new budget draft, about what it will say, about what she'll do if it says X, what she'll do if it says Y. "I'll see what I can see," she says. "Tell me if you figure out what's going on with Bradley."

The plan is to drive to Genova's, talk with Sam about the protest, order sandwiches to go, and take them home for dinner with Robert and Linda. They're trying Sam last because of the sandwiches, yes—so they're fresh for dinner, the buns not yet soggy with condiment moisture—but also because Sam feels easiest. Sam they really know.

They sit at the same booth where yesterday she left Bradley eating his turkey-and-bacon sandwich. Sam wants to know how Michael's doing, how their jobs are going, whether they noticed the new eggplant parmesan sub. He starts telling them about all the experimentation he did, all the different eggplant recipes, testing not just how they tasted but how they sat through the day, how they reheated, how they interacted with his bread. Yes, he says, he read the article they sent over. "Heavy stuff, guys. Very heavy."

She can tell Art is waiting for her, the one who knows Sam better, to move the conversation along. But she's too exhausted; when Art realizes this, he takes over. She closes her eyes and beams him her thanks, hoping he can feel it. He starts telling Sam about the protest, how they're looking to "raise awareness" and "start moving the needle a little if we can." The usual phrases.

"Hold on," says Sam. "Hold on, hold on. Am I guessing correctly that you're about to ask for my support? Like to sign something, or put a sign up, or—"

"Something like that," says Art.

"But the thing of it is," says Sam, "is that they're customers. The Arcadian people. They order all the time. I don't know anything about . . . We just drive up to the gate. They're regulars. They tip well. And that's all I know about it. I'm not in the business of—or what I mean to say is, this is a business. A small-town business. I can't be out in the street taking stands against my customers. Do you understand?"

Later, Mel won't be able to recall much of the conversation that follows. All she will remember is sitting in the back booth and taking in the inside of Genova's not as a place she knew she would be returning to but as one she was observing for the last time. It's not a decision she's actively weighing. It's a shift that already happened. She will never eat another Genova's meal. She ate her last Genova's egg salad sandwich without knowing to savor it. They need to figure something else out for dinner tonight. Robert and Linda are due in less than an hour.

The solution ends up being to go to the grocery store and buy the ingredients for simple quesadillas: tortillas, cheese, salsa, a rotisserie chicken. Greens for a salad. When they were first together, they went grocery shopping together all the time, for fun. Maybe they will start doing it again, now that Michael's gone.

Everyone in the store is staring at them.

She knows that can't actually be true, but still.

Everyone in the store has read the *Times* article or not read the *Times* article, heard something about it or not, seen the photographs or not seen the photographs, talked or not talked about them, does or doesn't get a paycheck from Arcadian Airlines.

She notices herself taking items from the shelves she doesn't need for dinner. A box of mac and cheese, a can of pinto beans, a jar of spicy mustard. All things they have at home. When she pays, she accidentally uses her business credit card. The mistake makes her more upset than it should. Art tells her it doesn't matter. She feels like she might cry.

Over dinner Robert and Linda say all the right things. They say how awful it is. They say they can't imagine what it would feel like. They don't jump into strategizing about what to do next, how to change Sam's mind, any of that. Linda doesn't talk about how messed up Springwater is or reminisce about the Klan rally or the old rusted-out sign, doesn't mention Iraq or how they stopped being activists. "We understand completely that you might not want to physically be there on Saturday," Robert says. "We understand completely."

Art gives her a *Well?* look.

"We'll be there," she says.

Linda takes out a flyer.

NO TORTURE ANYWHERE,

NO TORTURE FLIGHTS IN NC!

THE YEW COUNTY AIRPORT IS A CRIME SCENE!

JOIN US FOR OUR FIRST PROTEST,

THIS SATURDAY @ THE AIRPORT.

SEE NCATAN.ORG FOR DETAILS.

There are other versions, Linda says, that say nothing about the protest. "You'd know best which ones to put up. And where."

"Or if they should go up at all," says Robert. "We know you know best."

She clears the dishes and they sit around the table. Art starts talking, with no prompting, about how, for him, the journey away from activism almost certainly had something to do with his job. Being a full-time mental health worker, he says, turned out to be more consuming than he'd ever imagined it would be: the immersion, hour after hour, in other people's perspectives and problems. It was valuable in exactly the way he'd hoped it would be—he still feels that— but it wore him out. Over time, and without fully realizing it was happening, he came to think of each hour of his life as either *work time,* when he was devoting his energy to problems other than his own, or *off time,* when he took care of himself and his family, recharged his batteries, and in that way ensured he could keep going.

Robert says he thinks that's common. Common and completely understandable.

"And you were raising Michael, too," says Linda. "We had more time on our hands." She asks if they think they might have chosen differently about Iraq if Michael had already been off at college. Or whether they might be choosing differently now if Michael were still home. She's not criticizing, she says, she's just curious. There's not a right or wrong answer, or if there is, she doesn't claim to know it.

"Maybe," says Mel. "I'm not sure." In truth, all she remembers about not protesting Iraq is this: they got action blast after action blast and never gave any serious thought to attending a protest. That's it.

"Of course," says Linda, "there's your school board work, too. Which is like activism, isn't it? I really hope this isn't the end for your breakfast idea. That would be so sad. Will you let us know what we can do to help?"

"Of course."

"I mean it. We mean it. Don't we, Robert?"

"Absolutely," he says. "Absolutely."

They talk about their old houses, memorable gatherings they held, people they knew there and what became of them. Everyone but Robert, who will be driving, decides to have another beer. Two is a lot for Mel. It's the closest she's felt to Carlson Street in a long time. Since they left. She's in the kitchen looking for crackers when Linda launches herself up off the couch and shouts, "Music! We need music!" She thumbs through their CD shelf. "Don't you remember how much music we used to listen to, how we had music on all the time?" She loads up the CD player—Neil Young, Sam Cooke, Paul Simon, Richie Havens—and starts dancing, pulls Mel up from the couch so she'll dance, too. To her own surprise, Mel goes along with it. Robert and Art stay on the couches; she can hear them talking. Robert's asking Art what kind of music Michael likes. Art says he's not sure, he wishes he knew, he'll ask him the next time they talk. Robert says he always asks his students what they listen to and it's not all good—"I mean, it's not all for me"—but he likes a lot of it, and he likes the conversations, they make him feel less old. He's been wanting to design a course on the history of music and politics, but he hasn't had the time. Mel hears all this, but it doesn't interfere with her dancing, it's just wallpaper. "Dance with us!" says Linda, but it's clear she doesn't care if they do or don't, and soon they're winded and need a break anyway.

The conversation turns back to the flyers: where they might put them up, which businesses might accept them, which public spots might work. Mel can remember, in the old days, going around Durham, Raleigh, Chapel Hill—often with Linda, making an afternoon of it—stopping in coffee shops and record stores, stapling flyers on crowded bulletin boards on all the college campuses, talking to people, answering their questions. Now she can't think of a single place to put a flyer in the town where she's lived for so long. But maybe it's because she's slightly drunk.

"If you want," says Robert, "you don't have to deal with the flyers. You could tell us where they go and we could do it. If you want, I don't know . . . an extra degree of separation."

"No," she says. "No, no. No."

They drive downtown in separate cars. "In case we have to split up and flee," says Art with a wink. They park by the hardware store and walk, Mel carrying the flyers in a tote bag from work, Linda holding a roll of poster tape, all four of them speculating softly about this spot versus that one, this lamppost versus that traffic light support pole. Together, they create the downtown Springwater that people will see tomorrow. When they pass Genova's, Mel entertains the idea of taping a flyer—or multiple flyers—to the door for Sam to find when he arrives in the morning. They have enough to cover the whole thing.

"Did he say how long he's been catering for Arcadian?" says Robert. "Do you think it was happening while you were working here?"

She says he didn't say. She wishes she'd asked. She wonders if, over the summer, Michael ever delivered sandwiches to Bob Fox Road.

As they're hugging goodbye, she has the urge to say, *Don't go, not yet, come back to the house, let's have another beer, let's stay up like we used to, talking and talking and talking.* She doesn't want to go home, she's not tired, she wants them to drive, to find some other adventure. An all-night diner. The ocean. Anywhere, if they go there together.

But it's late. There's work tomorrow. They promise they'll talk tomorrow. They get in their cars. On the way home, she makes a wish that when they get home Michael will be there, happy to see them, ready to tell her why he came home that night, what he'd wanted to tell her.

But they get home and he isn't there. Of course he isn't. She puts the music back on, hoping to rekindle the mood, and it works for a little; she asks Art to dance with her and he does. She asks why he didn't dance before, when Linda and Robert were there. She asks if he was embarrassed.

"I was talking to Robert," he says.

"Sure, but—we should dance more often, don't you think?"

"Anytime," he says. "Anytime at all."

AYOUB

One day, on an impulse, he leaves for work early so that, on his way, he can visit the web cafe down the street. To his surprise, he likes it, and when he leaves he's already making plans to return. He likes the soft nods of the Somali brothers, and the solemnity with which they bring him his complimentary tea. He goes back the next morning, and the next. The better he gets at googling, the more he likes it. He reads about shoes that make working on your feet less painful; about stretches for back pain relief; about how to keep rescue cats healthy; about recipes for people with digestion problems. He dips into the endlessly self-expanding ocean of football updates: scores, transfer rumors, league developments. He never really considered himself a football person, and he still doesn't, but there's something nice about the ritual. Amira's father doesn't email or text, and speaking on the phone sounds awkward, but he starts saving up football-related observations for the next time they talk.

Later that week, at the end of his shift, Walid asks if he's heading home and, if so, whether he can walk with him at least part of the way.

"Of course," he says. What else is he supposed to say? He

knows what he's about to hear: that it's not working out, that Walid can't afford to keep him on for this or that reason, that he's fired. He's trying to figure out how to tell Walid that he doesn't mind taking a pay cut, that he doesn't need to be paid any more than anyone else at the stall, that he would even accept being paid less than everyone, if only he can stay.

In fact, Walid wants to know if he's interested in taking on more hours—"not on Sunday or Tuesday, of course"—and more responsibilities: if he wants to learn how to decide what to order from suppliers, how to process a delivery, how to modify pricing throughout the day, throughout the week, throughout each season. "You've done well," he says. "You really have."

He has the urge to keep the news from Amira until he actually proves he's able to do everything Walid thinks he can. But he overrides the reflex and tells her that night, because it's the right thing to do.

"Will you get paid more?"

"Of course. I'll be working more."

"Not more total. More per hour."

He's forced to admit not only that he doesn't know but also that he didn't think to ask.

"Hmm."

From the look on her face, he thinks he knows what she's thinking: that his wage to date has been a matter of pity, and this proves it.

"Well, maybe he'll get his money's worth now," he says. "Right?"

"I'm sure he will," she says. "I am proud of you, though."

"You are?"

"I am."

"I might need some new shoes. If I'm going to stand longer. I've been researching shoes. Online."

"Well, let's get you some."

More hours means taking shifts with Walid's nephew, the mean one, from the day he came to ask for a job; his name, it turns out, is also Walid. Now that they're coworkers, this younger Walid treats Ayoub pleasantly, striking a perfect balance—in word choice and tone—between formal language that communicates respect and informal language that communicates intimacy, that they're in it together. Does he even remember their first interaction? He notices when Ayoub starts wearing his new shoes and compliments him on the choice. He's a football fan, and Ayoub starts using him as a test audience for observations gleaned from his reading online. He even starts watching occasional games at home, developing a taste for their carefully calibrated mix of variety and sameness: every game of football is a game of football, and every game of football is different.

Finally the inevitable happens. In the middle of a rush, trying to maneuver around Walid—old Walid—while also carrying a box full of apples, he loses his balance and almost drops the whole box, which he saves, but only with a lunge forward that he can't control and that results in the box of apples ramming into a box of squash (a box that should have been unloaded by now but hasn't been), which slides off the table, the squash should tumble out and get bruised and broken and dirty, get stepped on, get wasted, but they don't, because Walid—young Walid—sees it happening and intercepts the box just as the squash are starting to roll out and reverses the process and lifts the box triumphantly above his head, like a goalie who's just intercepted a shot and, by doing so, saved the game. Because it's such a busy rush, at least a dozen people, and probably many more, see Walid pull it off; they clap and cheer, and once he's set the squash box down, he takes a low, theatrical bow.

"I owe you," Ayoub says, in Italian.

"You really don't, brother," says young Walid in Arabic. "Really, don't worry. There's no owing."

At the web cafe he sips tea and watches compilations of impressive goalie saves. He looks at pictures of Mourad's family in Spain. He researches cat carriers and tips about how to bring cats with you in cabs and on trains. He writes to Sarah, by way of her firm's translation service, and asks if there's any way to let the Red Cross know that he doesn't want any more of his letters delivered. He appreciates their efforts, he says, and he doesn't mind having the letters—if there even are more letters—sent to Sarah's office, in case they happen to contain any information of possible relevance to a legal case, whether his or anyone else's. *I have to warn you,* he writes in Italian, working on this single sentence for over ten minutes, *that I suspect any letters are unlikely to contain anything of real significance, just thoughts I allowed myself in dark times and wish I had never written down.* He asks her not to mention his request to Amira. He thanks her for all her help. He tells her he got promoted at work, and it feels true—even though, as Amira suspected, he isn't getting paid more per hour.

The next morning he has a response from Sarah: she's going to talk to someone at the Red Cross and see what she can find out.

On his last day, when the guards came to take him away, there was no warning. Yusuf was nowhere in sight and he had to go. Why now? He had no idea. There was no time to say goodbye the way he would have wanted to, person by person. It was one big goodbye: everyone shouting and stomping and clapping, which happened sometimes, the whole cell block exploding with the hope that if one person could walk out, everyone could walk out, plus also the hope that Ayoub was really going home, the guards said he was but the guards were liars, every word that came out of a guard's mouth was possibly a lie. None of them had ever seen what happened to someone who'd walked out. None of them had ever heard from anyone who'd left. They shouted and stomped and made the shouting and banging a prayer and Yusuf probably hid from the noise in one of his many hiding spots, and he never got to say goodbye.

He has no memory of his flight home. The few times that he tried to access it, he ended up stuck in the memory of another flight, the first flight, Pakistan to Morocco, the feel of the headphones on his ears and the goggles around his eyes shutting out everything besides the sensation of the jumpsuit on his skin, and the diaper around him, the shackles around his wrists, the seat beneath him. When his bowels and bladder gave their signals, he called out asking if he could use the bathroom, but thanks to the headphones, he couldn't hear himself; after a while he wasn't sure he'd even actually asked, and so he decided to ask again, and this time, after a few seconds, he felt the right headphone move off his ear and heard a booming male voice say, in barely comprehensible American-accented Arabic, *No bathroom*. The headphone snapped back on his ear, and when he's stuck in this memory, it sometimes feels that what he's most stuck in is the question of whether the voice that said *No bathroom* was or was not one of the same voices from his cell in Pakistan. He goes back and forth. It was, it wasn't.

Was.

Wasn't.

Wasn't.

Was.

Two weeks later Sarah writes back, via a translator. She's sorry, she says, that it took so long to get him an answer. But she has good news: the Red Cross has agreed to his plan. They've even created a new mail-redirection protocol, for anyone else who might, for any reason, want their mail redirected to their lawyers once they're home. *Thank you,* she says, by way of the translator, *for bringing this particular consideration to my attention.*

AMIRA

She keeps asking Meryem what he looks like when he's working at Walid's stall. Does he look happy? ("Not exactly happy, no.") Unhappy? ("That's not it, either.") Stressed? ("No, not stressed.") Worried? ("Maybe a little—but no, *worried* is too strong a word, I wouldn't say *worried*.") "Well, what does he look like? Tell me." Meryem says she's not sure what to say. She doesn't know how to describe it. In the end, she says that the main thing she's noticed is that Ayoub looks like he's trying very hard not to drop anything.

"So . . . stressed?"

"No, not stressed. Just focused. He looks really focused."

"Is he able to have children?" her mother asks on the phone.

"What do you mean?"

"I'm just curious. I don't know what they did to him. Can he still—"

"Yes, Mother. Not that it's any—"

"I'm just asking. It's a reasonable thing for a mother to ask."

"Okay, well. Now you know."

For the next two hours she's furious at her mother for presuming it's any of her business, then furious at herself for not actually knowing the answer.

. . .

On a Tuesday, he asks if she feels like taking a picnic to the Appian Way Park.

"Let's go somewhere closer," she says.

"But it's your favorite."

"It's okay, really. Let's just go somewhere closer."

"I don't want to go somewhere closer," he says. "I want to go to the Appian Way Park."

"Well, okay. If that's what you want."

"You don't like it anymore?"

"No, it's not that," she says. "I want you to pick something that works for you."

"In that case," he says, "I want to go to the Appian Way Park. The Tor Marancia section."

On the bus he takes the window seat and looks out at the city like a content child. She wonders to what extent he's doing so self-consciously, offering up his contentment as proof of how well he's doing, proof that she doesn't have to worry. She doesn't want to have these thoughts, she tells herself; she wants her mind to stop; she wants her mind to be still. If she could snap her fingers and make these questions stop coming, she would.

Once they're at the park, he asks what she feels like doing.

"You pick," she says.

"My pick," he says, "is for you to pick."

If it's really her choice, she says, then what she'd like is to walk a little. They keep a decent pace; she can't tell who's setting it and who's following, but Ayoub seems fine. His eyelids relax down some—not shut, just down—and he tilts his head up slightly and smiles as the sun caresses his face. It's a different smile than she's ever seen him make before, but unlike on the bus, there's no doubt in her mind that he's really smiling. She wants to be that relaxed. *Relax*, she silently orders herself, *relax, relax, relax*. When they sit for lunch, he doesn't eat much—probably, she suspects, for fear of having to use the bathroom before they get home. She tries to enjoy the food she made. She tilts her head up into the sun. It's the same sun that's shining on Ayoub, so it should be able to do for her what it's doing for him.

She starts telling him about coming here on her own: how it made him feel closer but also farther away, the pain (although she doesn't use that word) of feeling both at once. He asks if she ever went to their favorite coffee bar. She tells him she didn't, but that she often went to other coffee bars for late-in-the-day cappuccinos even though she couldn't afford them. "To feel close to you." She's trying to look right into his eyes but instead, against her will, alternating between his eyes and the grass.

"I love that," he says. "You know, if things keep going well for me at work, you could maybe start working less."

"I wasn't trying to make you feel guilty about money."

"I know. It's just something I was thinking about."

"Well, let's not worry about that now."

On their way back to the bus, he insists they stop at the coffee bar. She can see the plan forming in his mind: he'll order cappuccino for them both, as a gesture; he'll force himself to drink it; she'll feel sick with worry over what the coffee's doing to him as it works through his insides.

Instead, the waiter comes and Ayoub orders one cappuccino ("Despite the hour, I can't help it," he says) and one decaf tea ("for my wife"). She doesn't recognize the waiter. If he smirks, she doesn't notice it; maybe the owner—who may now be the former owner, who knows?—set a no-smirking-at-cappuccino-orders policy.

After the waiter leaves, Ayoub winks and tells her the cappuccino's actually for her, the tea's actually for him. "He can think *I'm* the dumb Arab," he says. "I don't mind."

"Ah."

"I just wanted to see you have one again, you know. They may not be for me right now, but I'm glad they're for you."

They sit there for a long time, much longer than they need to get through their drinks. When it's time to go home, their bus shows up almost twenty minutes late and so full of people that they can't get on.

"What's going on?" she says to Ayoub. "Is there something happening today we don't know about?"

He shrugs, and she can tell from the shrug that his back is hurting from all the standing at the bus stop. She's about to call a cab when another bus traveling the same line pulls up, completely empty. "What's going on?" she asks the driver. "What's happening?"

The driver refuses to be interested. "He was late," he says, pointing at the first bus, which is now a few cars ahead. "I'm on time. That's all I know about it. You want to know about him, you go ask him."

Ayoub picks seats near the middle of the bus.

"Is your back hurting?" she says.

"Yeah. Can you press it?"

"Press it how?"

"Press your hand on it."

"Where?"

He winces. "I don't know. I'm not—just try somewhere. Lower back."

She puts a hand on the small of his back. She never got used to how shrunken and fragile his back felt when he first returned—to get used to it, she would have had to touch him more—and she definitely isn't used to how it feels now, still smaller compared to before, but with new bands of tight muscle in unexpected places from his work at the produce stall, all the lifting and setting down and careful carrying. "Here?" she says.

"Lower."

"Here?"

"To the left. And lower."

"And then what?"

"Just—press."

"Like this?"

"Harder."

"Like this?"

"Harder—it feels good. Right there. That's good." She decreases the pressure and increases it again, and keeps repeating the cycle. "I wonder what the driver thinks we're doing." He's laughing before the sentence is even done, and then she's laughing, too. "Ow," he says. "Ow, it hurts. Don't make me laugh. No more jokes."

"I didn't make the joke."

"I know, I know. It's my fault."

For the first time in either of their lives as Romans, they have a bus to themselves for an entire journey. When they get in the apartment, Habiba comes lunging at him to play; he makes a soft clicking noise with his tongue and whispers, "Not now, sweet one. I'm tired. It's nap time." The cat actually does what he says, gives up on chasing them and walks across the living room and vaults up to the windowsill to look at the street below.

"I might nap, too," Amira says. "Should we nap together?"

She doesn't expect him to answer right away, and she doesn't expect him to say yes, and she wishes she hadn't asked. If he's tired, he should nap, nap where he wants to nap, put his body where it needs to be, not worry about her.

"Sure. Let's."

Because she never naps, she has no napping routine. She doesn't know what to wear or not wear. She doesn't know whether to set an alarm, or for when. She doesn't know what the cat will do; she can't have it in bed with them. If she shuts the door, what will Ayoub say? Will the cat paw at it? Make its sad noises? What will Ayoub do when he hears them?

But once they're both in the bedroom, he shuts the door and says—as if he's read her thoughts—that the cat will be fine.

And it turns out he's right.

MEL

On the Saturday before Thanksgiving, she and Art had just sat down to dinner when he told her, in the solemn tone of a doctor sharing unhappy test results, that he'd talked to Michael again that afternoon.

"Oh?" She and her son hadn't spoken since the day he hung up on her. Almost six weeks. She'd left him one voicemail—the night they put up signs downtown with Robert and Linda—but he hadn't called her back. She'd emailed to let him know he could call anytime, to talk about anything, big or small. *Okay, thanks,* he wrote back. She hadn't heard from him since; Art, meanwhile, had talked to him once a week. "And?"

"Well, he did finally open up some. About how he's doing. Some of the things we've been wondering about." The short of it, Art explained, was that Michael had found college more of a struggle than any of them—Michael included—had ever anticipated. He was homesick, the work was hard, structuring his time was hard; he'd known ahead of time to expect these challenges but, from what Art could tell, had made the mistake of assuming that this was the same thing as being immune to them. "Also, it seems he just hates his suite mates. Or seriously dislikes them—as suite mates, anyway. Maybe he'd think they were fine people in another context.

Apparently it's gotten really bad, though he was pretty vague about exactly how."

Art was speaking more slowly than usual, as if before each sentence left his mouth, he was putting it through a screening process, deciding what she should actually hear.

For a while, he said, Michael had tried to tough it out with the suite mates. Wait for a change. But a few days ago he'd gone to the housing office to talk about other options. "Which is probably a good thing, I think."

She cast her mind back to the day they helped Michael move in. All she could see through the fogged glass of memory was herself, Art, and Michael standing in a room—the suite's common room, probably—with three teenage boys they'd just met. Awkward, yes, but already slightly less awkward than just a few minutes before. There was relief in the air: they were no longer waiting to meet each other, their heads filled with every possible suite mate the universe might throw at them. Now they were real. Now they could begin.

"It won't always be like this," said Art. "This thing where he only talks to me."

"Yeah."

"It's just something he's going through."

They went back to eating. A reel of images unspooled inside her: Michael lying in his bed awake in the dark, listening to his suite mates laughing in their common room; Michael eating alone at a table in a corner of the cafeteria; Michael having his cafeteria dinner packed in Styrofoam so he can eat somewhere else, somewhere it feels easier to be alone; Michael wandering the fringes of campus, cell phone pressed to his ear, talking to Art but not her; Michael driving to Springwater that night, looking forward to her company, to the relief of home, pulling in and seeing an unfamiliar pickup in the driveway; Michael's keys scraping hard along the side of Bradley's truck.

"There was one more thing," said Art. They'd just sat down to watch TV; he was looking at the screen, not at her. "One more thing from Michael."

"Go ahead."

He looked like he wasn't quite sure where to start, or wished he didn't have to. Her stomach became a fist, squeezing.

"That stuff I told you about before. He said he wanted you to know. Wanted us both to know. But he doesn't want us making a big deal about it. He doesn't want us calling him about it, or asking lots of questions at Thanksgiving. He said he doesn't want us to freak out, and that he knows that's the exact kind of thing that makes parents freak out. But still, he doesn't want us freaking out. I think he's worried that if we make a fuss, he'll start feeling worse about himself. That's the idea, I think."

"But should we be freaking out? Are you freaking out?"

"I'm concerned," he said. "But trying not to freak out. I don't think we should freak out."

"Okay," she said. "I'll follow your lead. You're the one who talked to him."

"I'm sure he'll call you soon."

"Maybe."

"I'll tell him to."

"No, don't."

"Why not?"

"Just don't."

"Fine. I won't."

"Anything else? From your call?"

"No. That's it."

The day before Thanksgiving he arrived home just before noon. Right away Mel asked what he wanted for dinner. She'd taken the day off, preparation for the holiday meal was well underway, and she was ready to make her son whatever he wanted. "Anything," she said. "Your choice."

What he wanted—what he'd been looking forward to the whole drive home, he said—was Genova's.

She had no choice but to explain. "But you still can, if you want."

"Um. Does Sam even know? That you're boycotting him?"

"I don't know. He's probably guessed at this point. But I really don't mind if you go."

"What, I'll eat Genova's and you and Dad will have something else?"

"If that's what you want."

"No thanks."

"I'm sorry."

"Is this, like, a whole thing? Does everyone know about this?"

"Does everyone know that I don't eat Genova's anymore?"

"I mean, is this what you're, like, known for now? This protest?"

"I don't know," she said. "To some people, I guess." And it was true: she didn't really know. More than once, since the march at the airport, she had caught herself daydreaming about a machine that would somehow let her know what everyone in Springwater thought about her, about Arcadian, about the CIA, about the protest. Who thought X, who thought Y, who knew what, who knew nothing at all. Who had read the short article in the *Herald,* who had read the longer one in the *Independent,* who had looked up the *Times* article. The owners of the Benson house switched to another listing agent and didn't say why. Was it connected? A cashier at Walmart—someone she didn't recognize—stared at her while ringing her up, and spoke unusually slowly and loudly, and ended their interaction, bizarrely, by proclaiming, "God bless America." Was it connected?

"How about my pork chops instead?"

"Sure. Pork chops, good."

"You could go get Genova's now, for lunch?"

"I'm not going to do that, Mom. It's too awkward."

"I'm sorry."

"Stop saying that."

"But I am. For everything. I really—"

"I'm gonna go unpack, okay?"

"Sure, sure."

At dinner he seemed happy. It was a pleasure to have three people at the table again, a pleasure to watch her son enjoy her food, a pleasure not to be thinking about whether he was or wasn't going to call or email her, about whether she should or shouldn't call or email him, about what he had or hadn't said to Art. "I don't think I vary my diet enough," he said. "At school, I mean." She asked if the cafeterias didn't offer enough options. They did, he said, of course they did; he looked mystified by himself, but cheerfully mystified. He just had to make more of an effort, he said—that was all. Eat different things.

Her resolution for the whole weekend was simple: to figure out what her son wanted and needed from her, and to do exactly that.

Right now what he needed—as far as she could tell—was to sit at the table and eat her food and see that his parents were still together, and still happy. Which wasn't hard to show him, because it was true. They were doing more together than they had in years. Going to meetings in the Unitarian basement. Drafting letters and petitions. Planning a roadside vigil by the airport. Calling reporters, talking to reporters. Helping to answer emails that came through the website. They were seeing Robert and Linda all the time; just last week, they had dinner with Robert and Linda and four students from the Triangle Area Muslim Students Alliance and stayed up past ten in the living room, everyone telling stories from across their lives, making their worlds a tiny bit bigger. They were reading the same books. They were going on walks together. "Processing walks." "Strategy walks." They were having sex three or four times a week, a definite uptick.

She had meant to tell Art the truth. When she left Michael the voicemail saying that she already had, she knew, of course, that it wasn't literally true. She was a little buzzed—from alcohol but more from the mood of the evening, the thrill of putting up signs with their old friends—and she stepped into the backyard and dialed Michael's number and got his voicemail and it felt like the thing to say. She didn't think she was *lying*, not in any substantive way, because of course she was going to tell Art. She just hadn't had the chance yet, and waiting to hear was obviously hurting her son, and it was within her power to make the hurt stop, or at least blunt its sharpest edges.

She told herself she would tell Art before the march. Then she told herself it made more sense to tell Art after the march.

Then, after the march, told herself it made sense to wait a while. To not dirty his memory of the day. But of course it would be dirtied anyway, whenever she told him, wouldn't it? She told herself she would tell him anyway, and day after day she said nothing, and now they were together at the dinner table, and Michael seemed fine. Better than fine. The longer the meal went on, the longer they all sat there together, at the table where they'd sat together so many times before, the more it felt the way it used to. Easy and familiar. Michael helped clear the table, the way he always did. They worked together on loading the dishwasher while Art went to the bathroom. She assumed that what Michael wanted wasn't explicit talk about what had happened. He wanted—it was obvious, wasn't it?—for it to be over. Something he could forget. She asked which of his friends he was planning to see while he was home. In another part of her mind, she wondered what each of these friends knew, or thought they knew about her and Art and Arcadian. What they'd heard from their parents. What they'd say to Michael, what he'd say back. If, wherever it was his friends met up, he'd run into Paul, what Paul would say, or think without saying.

When Art came back, he told her to sit down and let him take a shift.

"Her?" said Michael, smiling to let them know his outrage was fake. A game he was inviting them to play. "Why not me?"

"Because," said Art. "If you go too long without doing dishes, you forget how."

"Fair enough."

She sat at the table and watched her husband and her son doing the dishes: splashing, snapping their towels, making jokes about each other's rinsing and loading techniques. She wished she had the camera on hand but she didn't and she wouldn't go get it because then who knew what she would miss. She could watch them forever and be happy, but she knew it wasn't possible, they would be done soon, and so while it was still possible to watch, she tried to do just that.

AMIRA

This year, Meryem doesn't invite her to come early to help set up for Nada's birthday party. Maybe she thinks Amira has enough to deal with now that Ayoub's home. Or maybe it isn't the result of any conscious thought process—maybe it just slips her mind.

Inside the apartment it's just like last year: same kids, same streamers, same table of food. The difference is that everyone's a year older. And Ayoub's here.

"Hello, hello!" It's Bouchra, heading toward them from across the room. She's so glad they're here, she says, she wants to hear everything about their little kitty, how she's doing, if there's anything she can do to help. Amira wonders: Does Bouchra remember staring at her with pure hatred in this very room exactly one year ago? Or has she wiped the memory away?

She leaves Bouchra and Ayoub and drifts away, looking for Meryem. The familiar awareness of being monitored jostles for space inside her with the awareness of Ayoub being monitored too. She watches (out of the corner of her eye) everyone watching (out of the corner of their eyes) Bouchra and Ayoub talking. He looks happy, of course he does, he could talk about Habiba all day.

Rounding the corner to the kitchen, she bumps into Nada.

They saw each other just a week ago, but today, the fact of her birthday draws Amira's attention to how much bigger and older the child is.

"Is Ayoub here?" Nada says.

"Yes, sweet one. He's talking to Bouchra in the other room."

"He wasn't here last year. He was in Morocco." Nada often says this type of thing when they see each other, as if repetition might make it more comprehensible to her. According to Meryem, she does something similar with the fact of her grandmother's recent death.

"That's right, yes."

"But now he's here."

"Yes. Isn't that nice?"

Nada nods solemnly. "Did he bring me a present?"

"I'm not sure. You'll have to ask him when you see him."

Another solemn nod and then she's off.

When Amira doesn't find Meryem in the kitchen, she heads back to the living room. Children run and shout and scream, parents pay half attention, someone's crying but it's nothing serious. She can't see Ayoub, and then she can: he's on the balcony, talking with Walid, laughing at something Walid's saying, genuinely laughing, it seems to her, not sucking up to his boss. When he sees her looking, he holds up a hand to pause Walid. He makes a gesture that she assumes means: *You're okay?*

She points at herself: *Me?*

He makes the gesture again: *Yes, you.*

She nods and gives a thumbs-up, and for a moment he returns to talking to Walid. But then he turns back and sees her still standing there, and again he puts his hand up—she can tell, through the glass, that he's apologizing to Walid, excusing himself for a minute—and then he's sliding the door open, and then he's walking toward her to come ask—it's like she can already hear it—how she's doing, if anything's the matter, if she's feeling okay, if she wants to leave. She stops thinking, for a moment, about who's watching them and what they might be thinking. She stands still, waiting for her husband to arrive from across the room.

This novel was inspired in part by the realities of extraordinary rendition and torture programs, including the lives of their victims and the activists who fight for them. I owe a special nod to the bravery, inventiveness, and perseverance of North Carolina Stop Torture Now. All of the characters in these pages, however, are entirely my own creation; their thoughts and actions, virtues and shortcomings, do not correspond to any real organizations or individuals.

A NOTE ABOUT THE AUTHOR

Peter C. Baker's writing has been published by *The Guardian, The New York Review of Books, The New Yorker, The New York Times Magazine, The Point,* and *Granta.* He lives in Evanston, Illinois.

A NOTE ON THE TYPE

The text of this book was set in Freight Text Pro Book, designed by Joshua Darden (b. 1979) and published by GarageFonts in 2005. It was inspired by the "Dutch-taste" school of typeface design and is considered a transitional-style typeface. Legible, stylish, and sturdy, Freight Text was designed to be highly versatile, belonging to a wide-ranging "superfamily" of fonts, including many versions and weights.

Composed by Digital Composition
Berryville, Virginia

Printed and bound by Berryville Graphics
Berryville, Virginia

Book design by Pei Loi Koay